Coming s

DEATH ON BLACK DRAGON RIVER
by Christopher West

"Not only an ingenious whodunit but an inquest into the Cultural Revolution and the violence it did to a generation. Skillfully assembled with people and places vividly rendered and history speeding through the narrative like adrenaline."
— Philip Oakes, *Literary Review*

"A wonderfully descriptive tale which evokes a convincing picture of everyday life in the new China. It is also a very good traditional mystery."
— *Deadly Pleasures*

"Absorbing . . . a first-rate mystery . . . but also a beautifully drawn, vivid study of a rural community riven by class hatred and haunted by the memories of events of a generation earlier."
— *Hampstead & Highgate Express*

"Inspector Wang follows a believable agenda played out against richly detailed backdrops that leaves the reader eager for new chapters in his career."
— Barbara Peters, *The Poisoned Pen*

DEATH OF A
BLUE LANTERN

Christopher West

BERKLEY PRIME CRIME, NEW YORK

DEATH OF A BLUE LANTERN

A Berkley Prime Crime Book / published by arrangement with
the author

PRINTING HISTORY
HarperCollins British edition / 1994
Berkley Prime Crime edition / August 1998

The Penguin Putnam Inc. World Wide Web address is
http://www.penguinputnam.com

ISBN: 0-425-16408-X

Berkley Prime Crime Books are published
by The Berkley Publishing Group,
a member of Penguin Putnam Inc.,
200 Madison Avenue, New York, NY 10016.
The name BERKLEY PRIME CRIME and the BERKLEY PRIME CRIME
design are trademarks belonging to Berkley Publishing Corporation.

PRINTED IN THE UNITED STATES OF AMERICA

10 9 8 7 6 5 4 3 2 1

for Mandy

AUTHOR'S NOTE

Many people have helped with this book, Western and Chinese. My heartfelt thanks to them all. If I do not produce a list it is because a) somebody always gets left out and b) Colonel Yue's real-life colleagues might not approve.

I have used the Pinyin system of romanizing Chinese characters, as that is the one currently used in China. It looks fearsome at first sight, but a few rules soon simplify it:

Q	is pronounced	Ch
Zh	is pronounced	J
X	is pronounced	Sh
-ian	is pronounced	-yen
-ong	is pronounced	-ung.

Thus Inspector Zhao is spoken 'Jao' (the -ao sounding like the exclamation 'ow!'), Xun Yaochang 'Shun', Professor Qiao 'Cheeow' (and so on).

Chinese surnames are put first. Ren Hui's daughter is Ren Yujiao.

LIST OF PRINCIPAL CHARACTERS

Number 6 investigation team:

CHEN	Team-leader
WANG Anzhuang	Inspector
ZHAO	Inspector
FANG	Sergeant
LU	Constable, Wang's assistant

Other CID personnel:

CHAI	Librarian at CID headquarters
LIU Qiang	Inspector investigating Triads
DA	Army Colonel, attached to CID
WEI	Party Secretary
YUE	Colonel in ISB (Secret Police)
HONG	Constable

Others:

XUN Yaochang	Petty crook
MENG Lipiao	Petty crook
REN Hui	Big-time gangster
REN Yujiao	("Jasmine") His daughter; sings at Qianlong Hotel
ZHENG, 'Eddie'	Floor manager, Qianlong Hotel
LIN, Rosina	Nurse at International Peace Hospital
Professor QIAO	Senior archaeologist, Huashan dig
Dr. JIAN	Her assistant
HEI Shou	Political chief, Huashan dig
WU	Chief Security Officer, Huashan dig
FEN	His assistant
PAO Xueyi	Cantonese customs officer
WONG, Lily	Hong Kong bar-hostess
LIM, George P.	"Overseas Chinese" policeman, on holiday in China.
LI Dehong	Senior manager at Qianlong Hotel
CHAO	His assistant
"BAI Lifan"	Alias assumed by Wang
ZONG Dingfu	Triad member

He who is great of spirit disciplines himself with humility. Ever modest, ever retiring, he fords the greatest river.

—*I Ching, Hexagram 15*

PROLOGUE

The Dragon King smiled, cracking his swirling mask of red and black. He sang; his voice soared up and down the musical scale like the roller coaster in the Cultural Park. He spoke, spitting out whole groups of syllables like a machine-gun then taking one and toying with it endlessly, till all possible meaning had been shaken out of it. The Witch Queen simply watched, nodding her head and sending long ripples up the pheasant feathers of her headdress. Then a cacophony of drums, woodblocks and gongs exploded from the wings. An apparently armless acrobat saltoed across the forestage; two men with wooden swords entered stage right and began slashing violently at one another. The air rang with the din of tramping feet, of ululating percussion, of crazy, keening voices.

Inspector Wang Anzhuang of the Beijing Central Investigations Department squeezed on to a wooden bench near the back of the auditorium and breathed a sigh of relief. He only went to the opera once a month, but work always seemed to make him late—last time he'd had to type up some ludicrous report for Team-leader Chen; this time it had been a call from an "informant" telling him a whole lot of things about the Huashan thefts that he knew already. This thought made him angry, and he lit a cigarette to calm himself down. It was a

Panda, for Party members only. Almost everyone else in the audience—mainly old men with close-cropped hair, work-wrinkled faces and gap-toothed grins—would be smoking stuff like Flying Horse: real throat-rotters. Many of them would have been working all day on hot, noisy, monotonous factory floors. Wang inhaled deeply and reminded himself he was lucky to have his desk, his perpetual refills of green tea, his status symbol pocketful of pens—not to mention his Type 77 service revolver as a memento of past action and adventure.

The on-stage action subsided. An ingénue began to sing, alone except for an *erhu*, a two-stringed violin that had been played in Wang's home province of Shandong for thousands of years. The inspector felt his heart wrench: the scraping fiddle and the lilting, lovelorn voice created a feeling of exquisite melancholy.

Lucky? Everyone in this room was lucky, to know and love this music, to share the culture from which it came—to be Chinese, to belong.

The inspector finished his cigarette and stubbed it out on the floor. Recently a Party directive had advised members to cut down on smoking for health reasons. But what did Tsao Tsao, his favourite soldier-poet, say?

"Drink and sing! How long is life?"

The players stood on the stage applauding the audience: the performance was over. The audience replied by stampeding for the doors, not from disrespect but necessity—last buses ran early, many had long cycle rides home, their factories would want them back at work at six next morning. Wang, with a Party flat in the centre of town, could take his time, relax and let the piece replay itself in his mind. Only when the hall was empty—apart from a drunk who had fallen asleep in the back row and two cleaners swishing brooms across the floor by the front exits—did he get up and walk slowly out into the narrow alley outside.

Dazhalan Street was always busy. Wang pushed his way through a throng of late-night vendors and shoppers. A woman held out a T-shirt with Chairman Mao's face on—once this would have been sacrilege, but now, in 1991, it was good business. A honeymoon couple—from the countryside, look at their sunburnt faces—held calloused hands and posed for a photographer. Music blared out of a clothes shop: *Careless Whisper*, one of the few Western tunes Wang knew and didn't dislike. A man selling deep-fried dough-sticks from a trolley bellowed his wares. The crisp, clean, morning-fresh smell had the inspector reaching in his pockets for a two-jiao note.

But it was no use. The image wouldn't go away. There had been something very strange about that sleeping figure in the back row, something that, as a policeman, Wang had a duty to investigate. He sniffed the cooking again, sighed and turned on his heels.

By the time he re-entered the auditorium, the sweepers were halfway to the back; they had built two mountains of rubbish and were working hard—and noisily—on the third. The figure was still leaning against the rear wall, his head at the same slight angle, his hands still by his side, and his complexion still as white as noodle-flour.

"Are you all right?" Wang called out.

No reply.

He made his way up the row and shook the fellow by the shoulders. The head moved only stiffly. He took his plastic-covered police ID and held it up to the fellow's mouth. Not a droplet of breath.

He didn't even try resuscitation.

For a moment, Wang thought of phoning the authorities anonymously. He wanted to go home and get some sleep: night staff got paid night rates; they could come and sort this out. But his sense of duty, that shadow companion of Tsao Tsao's drinking and singing, rebelled, just as it had done out on the street. Just as it always did.

One, check the body for foul play. Not that that was very likely, here at the opera. Two, search for—

Wang stopped, dumbfounded. At the back of the man's neck was a small hole surrounded by dry, black blood.

1

"It's a disgrace!" said Team-leader Chen, thumping his desk.

Wang shrugged. "I found the body."

"So what?"

"That makes me uniquely placed to solve the crime."

"You're part of a team. My team." Chen gestured round the grey-walled office at the other policemen present—Inspector Zhao, Sergeant Fang, Constables Lu, Tang and Han. "You can't just walk off cases when you feel like it. In all my time in the force—"

"Those are my orders," Wang cut in quickly. "To investigate the People's Theatre murder. Starting today."

The team-leader stared down at the pile of papers in front of him. "The Huashan operation is of national importance. Your role in it is essential."

Wang grinned to hide his embarrassment. His role was coordinator, a grand title which actually meant he stayed at HQ checking background information and manning a phone-line. It required very little intelligence and even less initiative—and was exactly the sort of dead-end job he'd been getting for the last couple of years. Due to age, he kept telling himself.

"Thank you, Comrade Chen," the inspector said cautiously. "But given the steady progress being made at Huashan, I feel

I can safely delegate my work here to one of the constables. It will be good experience for them."

The first part of this statement was a lie: the investigation, into a series of thefts from an archaeological dig in the mountains north-west of the capital, was getting nowhere. But it was the right kind of lie, official-sounding and optimistic. It seemed to work on his boss, who nodded his head and muttered: "Steady progress . . . Yes, I believe that sums up the situation well . . ."

"I'll be working from here, too," Wang went on. "So if anything arises while I'm present, I can assume control."

Chen nodded again, then picked up a sheet of paper. "It says here I'm to second a constable to you."

Wang stayed silent. Chen couldn't object: orders were orders.

"Take Lu," said the team-leader. The two other constables, older, more experienced men, showed no emotion, though Wang guessed they would be amused.

"I want you both back on my case within a month," Chen went on.

"A month?"

Wang gritted his teeth. Team-leader Chen had lost enough face already: if the murder were a relatively simple affair, Wang should easily have it cleared up in that time. If not, then he could make a direct appeal to the Unit Party Secretary, "Hawk" Wei. Not something Wang relished, but if it were necessary . . .

The inspector retired to his own cramped, airless office, where he piled up all the papers relating to the Huashan operation, carried them across to a corner and dumped them there. As he turned to face an empty desk he felt a surge of excitement: a case of his own again.

The two men stood in the mortuary, Wang in his olive-green police uniform with bright gold and blue epaulettes and yellow ribands, Dr. Zhang in a grey overall smeared with blood. Beside them, the corpse of the victim lay naked and white under a sheet.

"The weapon was a small, sharp knife," said the doctor. "The killer knew what he was doing. One insertion, severing the medulla; death was almost instantaneous. No shouts or screams, and very little blood.''

"Much force needed?"

The doctor shook his head. "Just skill. The assailant could have been male or female, young or old.''

"Any clues from the angle of the wound?"

"Some. The killer was probably about average height, right-handed and sitting on the victim's left. But when I say probably, I mean probably.''

Wang nodded. "Time of death?"

"Around seven-thirty.''

"Not later?''

"I don't think so. We can't be a hundred per cent accurate.''

"No . . .'' Wang had guessed as much—rigor mortis takes at least an hour to set in—but would like to have been proven wrong. "So he must have sat there, dead, through most of the performance.''

"Unless someone brought him in later.''

"No. That *would* have attracted attention.'' Wang let his thoughts drift back to the theatre. "It's dark in those cheap, back seats. There's a fight scene on stage—noise filling the auditorium. I suppose it's a better place to kill someone than the open street. But not one I'd choose, if I were planning a murder . . . Any signs of a struggle?''

"No.''

"Hmm. So it was unexpected: he must have known and trusted his attacker. Interesting . . . Do we have a name for him yet?'' The victim had not been carrying any papers, only a dirty handkerchief and a Martial Arts magazine.

"I'm afraid not. The computers are down again.''

Typical. Wang pulled back the cover and stared at the corpse's scarred, moustachioed face. Late twenties. Tough-looking. Not your standard opera-goer, but so what? *Jingju*, Beijing Opera, was still a People's art-form. Anyone could attend; all sorts of people did.

But this one nameless, lifeless individual—why had he come? For pleasure? To meet someone? To escape from some-one? Or was this a pointless, random killing, the kind Wang read about happening in the West? He shook his head. No, there'd be a reason. Someone had wanted this man dead. Who? Why?

Constable Lu sat in the team office. Most of the morning, he had been typing a report on a slow, difficult machine that built up characters stroke by stroke. He was due a rest. His boss was next door, on the phone; Lu took out his latest mini-computer game, turned the volume down and began to play.

World Cup Football. Select two teams. China versus Brazil. Two sets of bandy-legged players began waddling across the little screen, passing a square ball to one another. Goal! China one, Brazil nil. Too easy—take it up a level. Damn it—one all.

"Working hard, Lu?"

"*Ai!* Yes, sir. Well, no, sir. I just started a minute ago, sir."

Wang knew he should get angry, but there was something about Lu that reminded the inspector of himself at nineteen. Not the youngster's slow-wittedness, nor his privileged background, but a simplicity of outlook, an openness. At forty, Wang had become like cut bone, polished horn, carved jade, ground stone.

"Who was that on the line, sir?"

"Technical. They've got us a name for our murder victim. Xun Yaochang. He's got a record, so I want you to check his files here. I'll go and do his *hukou*."

Lu grinned. *Hukou* records, kept at outlying police stations, are boring; the files in the HQ basement are full of murder, fraud, blackmail, conspiracy, counter-revolution . . .

"I want a report by three-thirty."

"Yes, sir." The young man jumped to his feet and lolloped out into the corridor.

Wang went back to his room, lit a Panda, tilted his chair back and gazed round: bulging metal filing-cabinets, dusty wall-maps, narrow head-high windows, a grey stone floor and, right opposite him, his calligraphy-scroll. Two characters in bold, free-flowing "Zen" style: *zheng yi*, justice. Wang had created them himself in the traditional manner, meditating on their meaning for an evening then picking up a weasel-hair brush and dashing them down in an instant. They were good, he knew that; solid but infused with life, just as justice itself should be . . . As he stared at them, his thoughts went back to Nanping village. He remembered his father, a passionate self-taught Communist, giving him the characters to study, along with the works of Mao and Marx. A man without values is just an animal, Old Wang used to say . . .

Young Wang took a deep drag on the cigarette and watched the smoke curl up towards the striplight on the ceiling. He felt a pang of guilt: was he being selfish, grabbing this case and letting his team colleagues battle on with the seemingly insoluble business at Huashan? "Bourgeois individualism," Old Wang would have called it, the sin of putting one's own desires above the general good . . . His eyes returned to the scroll. But what crime could be worse than the taking of life?

A group of little generals—round-faced boys in oversize People's Liberation Army caps and tunics that came down to their ankles—watched as the rider drew up outside Chongwen Number Two Police Station and parked his motorbike under a torn canvas awning. The Chinese police wear no badges of rank, and the boys tried to guess the status of the new arrival.

"He's just a sergeant," said one. "Look at that Happiness bike. If he were senior, he'd have a Japanese one."

"Perhaps he's in disguise," said another. "The head of the *Ke Ge Bo*, on a top-secret mission."

"You shouldn't call it that," said a third, whose father was a Model Worker. "It's proper name is Internal Security Bureau. I think this fellow is a superintendent."

The object of this discussion paused to glance at a poster—a cartoon account of a recently solved fraud case, whose last frame showed the fraudster kneeling on the ground, blindfolded, about to be executed—then carried on up the steps.

"*Hukou* office is on the left," the duty sergeant told him. "Second door down . . ."

Wang followed the instructions, and found a young constable in shirtsleeves filling in forms by the light of a bare bulb. Four great precipices of paper rose up round the room walls: *hukou* files, on everyone who lived in Number Two area—their work record, their family background, any reported misbehaviour, any close contact with outsiders, their visits (if any) to other parts of the country. There would be no exceptions, for without a file they couldn't get ration tickets for cooking oil, soap, clothing, noodles or rice.

"I want information on someone called Xun Yaochang," said Wang. "He was murdered last night."

The young man nodded with a cynical lack of surprise: Chongwen can be rough area. He checked the character *Xun* in a directory, crossed to the far corner and pulled out a file. Wang blew the dust off and sat in a corner reading. Xun Yaochang had an address in the worst part of the district, a patchy work record, a list of complaints by neighbours—drunkenness, playing loud music, repeated refusals to participate in voluntary campaigns. He had no recorded dealings with foreigners and had never applied for permission to leave Beijing.

"Did he sign for his ration tickets?" the inspector asked. "I'd like to see his signature."

"They're at the back." The young man came over and found him one dated 17th January.

"You don't get signatures every week, then?"

"We'd have queues going round the block if we did. We try and get them every three months or so; the previous signature should be around October. Yes, here we—oh." The constable grinned: the two signatures were totally different. "Maybe he's illiterate, sir. People do that, you know—get friends or relatives to sign for them."

"You should check," said Wang severely. Then he shrugged. "Never mind. The information's been useful."

He closed the file, and handed it back to the constable, who dropped it into a cardboard box.

"Dead people go downstairs," the young man explained.

"Xun Yaochang probably will," Wang replied, but the fellow didn't get the joke.

"I'm sure we told the police when he left," said Mrs. Wan. "We don't miss much round here. That boy on the *hukou* is useless. Constable Li knew us all by name."

Wang nodded. The retired folk who head Neighbourhood Committees were a varied lot. The best ones were kindly and experienced, giving their time freely to mediate in disputes, to care for the sick and to advise youngsters heading in the wrong direction. The worst ones were nosey, narrow-minded, petty and vindictive. Mrs. Wan looked to be one of the latter kind.

"It must have been at least six months ago," she went on. "If not more. Good riddance, too."

"So you didn't think much of him?"

"Much? He was a thoroughly bad element. Drinking, fighting, noise at all hours of the day and night. Girls used to come and stay the night at his flat, too. There's not room for two beds in that place of his. I looked in through the window once and—"

"Different girls or always the same girl?"

"Don't know . . . Different ones usually."

"Can you name any names?"

"No," she said angrily. "Go down Goldfish Alley—I'm sure you'll find them there."

Wang nodded. Goldfish Alley was the site of the capital's new red-light district.

"So you've no idea why Xun Yaochang left or where he went to?"

"No." Mrs. Wan suddenly broke into a smile, revealing her three remaining teeth. "What's he done, then?"

"Nothing."

The smile vanished. "He must have done something."

"It's a family matter."

"Hmph!"

"Tell me about Xun's work, Comrade. 'Businessman,' it says in his records."

Mrs. Wan scowled. "*Ai-ya!* We all know what *that* means. Chairman Mao was right. All capitalists are criminals. Look what they tried back in '89, in Tiananmen Square!"

Thirty-one Tinkers' Alley was Xun's last known address. The *hutong* was typical of the area: narrow, bumpy and surrounded by high, windowless brick walls, behind which were old Qing dynasty courtyards. These had once been the homes of rich officials and their retainers; now they were mass housing and going to seed. Number thirty-one looked typical—grimy and unwelcoming. Wang knocked at the thick wooden door; no one answered. He knocked again. A young man in a T-shirt, jeans and reflector sunglasses appeared.

"What d'you want?"

"I'm looking for a fellow called Xun Yaochang."

"Never heard of him."

Wang narrowed his eyes. "How long have you lived here?"

"I've got a residence permit."

"Glad to hear it. Now answer my question. How long?"

"'Bout four months."

"Ah. Mind if I come in and look around?"

"Haven't got much choice, have I?"

Wang stepped over the stone lintel into the long, dog-leg hallway: a second door took him into the courtyard itself, a plot of bare earth about ten feet square littered with rubbish. Wang knocked at a few doors and peered in through a few of the cracked, dusty windows. The rooms were untidy; he sensed he would not get much cooperation from their inhabitants unless pressure were put on them. Which it could be, of course, but that wasn't the way Wang liked to do things.

He lit another Panda and smoked it while the youth watched in silence, hands stuffed deep into pockets. Too many of the capital's young people were like this nowadays—self-absorbed, surly, passionless. Would they really throw away everything the previous two generations had fought, sweated and died for?

At the People's Theatre, a team had been questioning staff. The back row was still roped off: the floor around where Xun had sat had been cleared and the rubbish taken away for analysis.

"It seems the victim came alone," the sergeant in charge, a swarthy southerner called Ye, told Wang. "The woman selling tickets recognizes a photo. She thinks he's been here before, too. And I've spoken to a sweetseller, who saw him inside, talking to someone."

"Ah! What did this someone look like?"

"The witness didn't get a front view. Just the back of a head."

"Height?"

"About one metre seventy-five."

Wang nodded. Tall for a woman or a southern male; average for a Beijing man. "Age?"

"She's not sure. I said, she only got a back view."

"Clothes?"

"Jeans, grey Mao jacket and trainers—and glasses."

"Glasses?"

"She noticed the hook round his ears."

"I wish the rest of the public were that observant. Got many more people to interview?"

"The orchestra are coming back here at four—specially: there's no performance tonight."

Wang nodded. The theatre now only put on Beijing Opera once a week: all other days they showed foreign movies.

"You're doing well, Sergeant. Keep it up."

Wang walked back down Dazhalan, calling in at general shops to see if they sold pocket knives. Several did: Wang made a note to get the Sergeant on to these establishments, while at the back of his mind the sad truth registered, that these objects were clearly on sale all over the capital. If the murder had been planned, the killer would have purchased the weapon somewhere else. If he'd needed to purchase one at all . . .

Wang was back at HQ by three-thirty. Constable Lu was ready with his dossier.

"Xun Yaochang was a small-time crook," he told his boss. "He's suspected of involvement in various rackets: currency dealing, unlicensed street trading, handling stolen goods—"

"And convictions?"

"One for drunk and disorderly, one for stealing a bicycle—"

A recitation of minor offences followed. Wang listened, deep in thought, spinning a pen across the backs of his fingers like a propeller. Why kill someone like that?

"These rackets," he said slowly. "He works with others, I take it. Do we have any accomplices on record?"

"A few, sir. Someone called Wu Chengfa. Zhang Hua . . . There's a Meng Lipiao—"

The propeller stopped. "There's a name I know! Meng Lipiao, Monkey-face Meng! He'll have a story for us. If we can find him, that is . . ."

Wang's voice faltered. He began staring at the dusty, pin-pricked map on the wall.

"Of course! Lu, have you ever wanted to own a nice piece of Ming dynasty porcelain?"

"No, sir. I've always felt that antiquities are a common heritage and should belong to the People."

"How about one made in Shanghai last week?"

"I thought the Ming dynasty was a long time ago, sir."

Wang paused. Was it worth explaining? No. He grabbed his jacket and made for the door, beckoning the young man to follow.

2

The clocks on the huge brick towers of Beijing Main Station snapped round to the hour and a chime began to boom out the opening bars of *The East is Red*. A few rustic, wide-eyed faces lifted up to listen, but Beijingers had long since stopped taking notice of the old Maoist anthem. Wang simply checked his watch and began scanning the scene in front of him.

"Any sign of him, sir?" Lu asked.

"Not yet."

The young man shook his head. "Another false trail . . ."

"Patience, Lu. Patience."

The huge open space in front of the station was, as usual, crammed with people. Soldiers stood in groups, the young recruits holding hands like children. "Minorities" from the mountains and deserts of the west sparkled in their bright clothes and flashing jewellery. Han peasants from a million places like Nanping sat stockaded in family groups behind the big-city purchases that would give them so much face back home. Among this crowd moved the vendors and racketeers, selling food, magazines, soft drinks and black market seat allocations, buying Hong Kong dollars or Foreign Exchange Certificates for grubby rolls of People's Money. In a far corner, a man had set up an illegal game of ace-in-the-hole. He was calling for bets; the fellow in his audience perpetually upping the stakes was obviously a plant. Even so, several travellers had been sucked in. Another time, Wang might have gone and done something about it. Off duty, he might have joined in: today, however, Wang wasn't interested. None of the participants had a grin so like the hero of the old children's story, that a nickname was inevitable.

"Let's wander about a bit."

They walked across the front of the station and into its huge marble main hall. THE PEOPLE'S RAILWAY SERVES THE PEOPLE, announced a banner over the eighty-foot high map of China. An announcement cut into the soft folk music coming out of the tannoy. Like railway announcements all over the world, it was incomprehensible. More vendors: no Meng.

The policemen moved on, back on to the square then down a side alley full of teastalls and cheap noodle cafés. There was a bristle of resentment as the two officers walked by. They reached the long-distance bus park.

"Ah!" Wang pointed to a man in reflector sunglasses sitting on a wall, surrounded by nick-nacks. "I knew he'd be here!"

Lu began rolling up his sleeves.

"We're going to talk, Lu."

The young man's face fell.

"If you want some action, go and wait by the Metro entrance. If he tries to run away, that's the way he'll go. It'll be up to you to stop him . . . You've double-checked his recognition characteristics?"

"With a face like that?"

"Clothes, height, build, age, distinguishing marks . . ."

"Yes, sir."

Lu hurried off. Wang breathed a sigh of relief.

Meng Lipiao pointed to one of the objects on his tray. "That's worth two hundred yuan," he told the foreigner. "At least. Though I can let you have it for one hundred and fifty."

The customer—a backpacker, not a monkey but a bird, with a beak for a nose and goggling eyes—nodded. "Eighty?" he suggested.

"Eighty? This piece is two hundred years old. At least . . . One hundred and forty. People's Money. In the shops—" Then Meng froze. "Motherfucker . . ."

"One hundred?" the foreigner continued. "That's my limit."

Meng shoved the pot into his hands. "Ten yuan. It's yours. Take it!"

The foreigner scratched his head, reached for his wallet—then saw what Meng had seen. A Communist policeman. Heading his way. There was a tinkling sound as the pot hit the pavement.

"Hey!" Meng shouted as the customer fled in panic: he thought of doing the same, but Wang was too close.

"I've got a licence, you know, officer."

"I'm sure. For selling genuine goods at fair prices."

"You heard me. Ten yuan, I was asking that ghost-devil."

"Foreign friends, you call them nowadays." Wang picked up a bowl with a blotchy red glaze and looked at the markings on the bottom. "Xuande reign? That must be worth a bit."

The monkey grinned. Wang threw the bowl on to the pavement, where it broke into smithereens.

"Even by your standards that's rubbish," Wang said. He picked up another bowl and read the mark. "Tang dynasty? And it looks so new . . . Mind if I show it to a colleague in the fraud squad?"

Meng sighed. "How much d'you want?"

"Nothing."

"The last gold-badge was happy with ten yuan a week."

"I'm not interested in bribes. I want to talk."

"What about?"

"An old colleague of yours. Xun Yaochang."

A look of sheer terror flashed across Meng's face. "I don't know who you're talking about."

"You do . . ." There was a sudden hesitancy in the inspector's voice: why such a strong reaction?

"I don't."

"Yes, you do. It's on record."

"Well, I haven't seen him for years."

That was better. "That's not what it says in our files."

"Months, then. But I haven't seen him recently. I don't know anything about him."

"You're old colleagues."

Meng snorted in disgust. "We were. That's over. Look, I've

got nothing to tell you. Why don't you leave me alone?''

"I will. Once you cooperate."

"OK. But I can't be much help. I don't know anything about Xun. Now, that guy over there—''

Wang had been deskbound for too long. He glanced away for a second, and the edge of Meng's tray hit him in the side of the face. There was a crash of tumbling crockery; the huckster was away into the crowd. Wang, wrong-footed, was behind him. Too far behind.

"Stop that man!"

A group of boy soldiers watched gormlessly as Meng jinked past them.

"Stop that man!"

An old woman bravely reached out a hand; Meng swept her aside.

Then he was gone, swallowed up by the great sea of people.

Constable Lu leant against the wrought iron side of the Metro entrance, staring at the passers-by.

"Wang keeps so still when he watches," he said to himself. "Why can't I do the same?" He tried to, and a pop tune jingled into his head. He tried again, and a young Shanghainese woman strutted past in a short skirt and black stockings. He tried again, and an ice-cream vendor appeared with a barrow.

That was too much. Nothing was happening. Had Wang just been trying to get rid of him? Probably. The inspector did that sometimes . . . Lu joined the line, brought his lolly (a vanilla one, in the shape of a space rocket), pulled off the wrapper.

There was a commotion in the crowd ahead. Someone was barging towards him: a man in a leather jacket and jeans. Height about one metre seventy. Build—

The young policeman felt a rush of panic. Then overcame it, steadied himself, drew himself up to his full height—and realized he still had a lollipop in his hand. Meng spotted him and turned at once, back into the crowd.

Lu gave chase. He was young and very fit—a good Communist looks after his body—and was soon gaining on his quarry. Meng turned into an alley. Lu followed: Meng suddenly realized the alley was blind. He was trapped. He stopped too. The two men stared at each other.

What was it the inspector said about not getting people into impossible situations? How tigers fight when cornered ... Meng advanced towards him, suddenly bristling with aggression. For a second, the young man's courage failed and he took a step back—and Meng was running at him. Shamed by his weakness, Lu threw himself at the tiger. Meng crashed to the ground with a thud, let out a cry of pain, tried to get up, staggered a few paces—then Lu had handcuffs on him.

A small crowd of people gathered.

"What's he done?" said one.

"Criticized the government, probably," said another.

Then Inspector Wang arrived.

"All we want is some help," said the inspector.

"You've a bloody strange way of asking for it."

"You've an even stranger way of offering it."

Silence fell. "Why me?"

"I said. You were a colleague of his. Pretty close, by all accounts."

"Was. I'm not any longer."

"Why not?"

"No reason. We're just—not."

"You had a nice racket in stolen goods. What happened to it?"

"It stopped."

"Why?"

"Because it did."

"D'you want the proper interrogators in?" said the inspector, suddenly angry. "It could easily be arranged."

Meng glanced round at the room. Public Security HQ, Qianmen East Street: people could come in here and never come out again. He shook his head. "Xun tried to cheat me."

"When?"

"About six months ago."

"Aha. Tell us the story."

Meng glanced around again.

"There aren't any bugs here," the inspector said. "Lu, put that pencil down. This is off the record."

The constable looked surprised but did as he was told. Meng began to tell his story.

"Xun had got hold of a camcorder—a lovely one, a Sony, still in its box. Of course, I've no idea where he got it from; all I did was find him a client. That's business. Brokerage. We arranged to meet on a bus. The 352—they're pretty empty midday. The client and I sat at the back; Xun was to get on a few stops from the end. If all was clear, we'd do a swap there and then. If there were many other passengers, we'd go to a park near the last stop and do the swap there. Then Xun got on—with three other guys."

Meng shook his head, then continued. "He told us to go to the park. So we did. Then he pulled a knife on us, took the camcorder, my client's wallet, even our shoes. Bastard!"

The inspector nodded. "And you haven't seen him since?"

"No."

"You must want to get your own back!"

"Yes. I mean, no. You know the phrase, officer: 'the past is like smoke.'"

"Acrid, all-pervasive and potentially lethal . . . Who were these three fellows?"

"Don't know."

"What did they look like?"

"Nothing special. Just toughs. There are plenty like that around."

"You seem to be particularly scared of these ones. Would you like to tell me why?"

"I'm not scared!"

The inspector turned to his subordinate and asked him to fetch some mugs of tea; the kid looked disappointed but did as he was told.

"I mean what I say about confidentiality," the inspector said once he and Meng were alone. "But I've also got a job to do. I could make things very difficult for you. If you leave me no choice. Who were those men?"

Meng began twisting and turning on his seat. The inspector watched him. Enjoying his discomfort? No. Just waiting. And waiting. In silence.

"How about this?" the policeman said suddenly. "I'll tell you what I think was going on, and you can correct me."

"OK."

"Your friend Xun got bored with pulling small jobs like camcorders and decided to move up in the world. Right? And those people on the bus were his new colleagues. This was a test of loyalty. Ditch an old friend for us . . . And I imagine you got a visit from them a few days later, telling you to keep quiet. How am I doing?"

Meng had never been any good at hiding his feelings.

"Now, I want the name of the gang and the names of any individuals you knew. Then you can go. None of this will ever be on the record. Of course, if you don't tell me . . ."

Meng glanced at the inspector's cold patient face, down at his own feet, at the cell door. Qianmen East Street.

". . . We could keep you in here for a long time."

The noise of the city came in through the window. Bicycle bells, klaxons, voices: people going about their everyday business. Freely.

"A very long time," the inspector said.

Meng held out his palm and traced three characters on it. *Yi Guan Dao.*

The inspector stifled a gasp. The Yi Guan Dao Triad hadn't been active in China since the fifties, since Chairman Mao had waged war on them. "Now tell me the truth," he said.

"I've told you the truth! You fucking dogs, you're all the same. I should have—"

The inspector held up a hand. "Just checking. Give me some names."

"I don't know. Really, I don't. Please stop this."

"You got a visit from the Enforcer, didn't you?"

Meng said nothing. He couldn't . . .

"So let's have his name."

"No. You must understand—"

"No one's going to find out." The inspector frowned. "And if you don't talk . . ."

More silence, more trapped-animal glances. Give a false name—but it was too late. The police knew too much already. Meng traced out the name of the Triad's 'Red Cudgel', their Enforcer.

"And the others?"

"I really don't know, Inspector. Please believe me. Haven't I said enough?" Meng was about to go down on his knees.

"OK, I believe you."

He sang back on his seat and wiped the sweat off his brow. The constable came back with the tea.

That was better. Meng gulped it down. "What's Xun done, then?" he asked in the cheeriest voice he could muster.

"Nothing."

"Nothing? You mean you've put me through all this—"

"He's been murdered."

Monkey-face Meng's eyes widened in astonishment. Then a shiver of fear ran through him. Then he burst out laughing.

Wang asked a few more, minor questions, then let his prisoner go. Meng was unable to supply much detail about Xun Yaochang's private life—he had no idea whether Xun was a regular opera-goer; he knew of nobody apart from himself who bore Xun a grudge, though he bet there were dozens. Wang gave him a phone number to call if he had any trouble with the Triad, and organized for an unmarked car to take him to within a few blocks of his home.

"There's our first suspect," said Lu, once Meng had gone.

Wang shook his head.

"He's got a motive."

"He was telling the truth. Very interesting truth, too . . ."

"Shall I write a report?" Lu asked.

"No. Best not."

Lu looked puzzled. Wang had taught him a lot about police work. Yet sometimes the old man broke basic rules . . .

Wang made his way down to the basement, where the CID library was based. He was hoping to find his old friend, "Wheels" Chai, a former undercover investigator who had been shot in the back by a gang of drug smugglers—but instead an assistant was on duty.

"If you'd like to fill in one of these forms, we can let you have five files to take away," she told him. "You are allowed to keep them for twenty-four hours, then you have to get clearance from the fifth floor."

There was a buzzing noise and Chai's electric wheelchair rolled into view.

"Young Wang!" The occupant held out a hand, and Wang shook it warmly. "What can I do for you?"

"I want all the information you've got on the Yi Guan Dao Triad."

"All of it?"

"As much as you can spare. And I want it for as long as I need it."

Chai nodded. "Miss Hu, give the inspector everything he needs."

The assistant glared back, opened her mouth to protest, then went off. *Guanxi*, contacts: they make the world go round.

"So what brings about your interest in the Triads?" Chai continued. "I thought you were investigating art thefts. Are the Yi Guan Dao involved in those?"

"No. It's a murder. Committed under my nose. Well, behind my back, anyway. Of a small-time hood whom we think joined up."

"Chopped to bits with meat cleavers, was he?"

"No, stabbed. But there's a link, so I need to follow it up."

"Ah. A bit like that business with the forged banknotes in Shanghai . . ." The two old colleagues began reminiscing until Miss Hu appeared with two armfuls of files.

"Those look heavy," said Wang. "Allow me . . ."

She glared at him. "I was runner-up in the all-China Police Athletics Association decathlon. I used to lift this weight fifty times a day. Where is your office?"

"Third floor."

"Follow me."

Wang did as he was told. Up in the office Miss Hu put the files on his desk, acknowledged the inspector's thanks with a curt nod and walked out. Wang grinned, embarrassed by his own mixed reactions of annoyance and admiration. Then he selected a file at random and began to read.

Investigations into the activities of the Yi Guan Dao Triad, by Inspector Liu Qiang.

He glanced up at the clock; half-past four. He'd just skim through the stuff now, then get home on time for once.

Next time he looked up, it was seven.

3

Wang closed the file and stared blankly at its drab grey cover. His head spun with the information that lay within it. According to Inspector Liu, the Yi Guan Dao Triad was back in force. They covered their tracks well—Ren Hui, the man Meng had named, was also a legitimate businessman active in import-export. There was no cast iron evidence to associate him with anything criminal, but Inspector Liu had become convinced that Ren was the Enforcer of a Yi Guan Dao lodge called the Green Circle, and had killed a fellow called Zhang Bei who had been found floating in the Tonghui River minus his feet and hands.

The Green Circle kept particularly good security. There was no information at all about its leader, except that he was referred to as the Shan Master. It was also known that the lodge was expanding—and, according to rumour, a swearing-in ceremony for 'blue lanterns' (new recruits) had been held about six months ago. Liu had even described what the ritual would be like.

To join a Triad meant to change your life, to die and to be born again—hence the name blue lantern: Wang still remembered the old custom of hanging lanterns outside the homes of the dead. The initiation ceremony was designed to impress upon the youngsters the totality of their new commitment.

Wang imagined Xun Yaochang going through it—Xun and probably four or five other young men, in grey, kneeling to receive burning incense sticks from the Shan Master, which they would then dash to the floor to simulate their fate if they broke the Triad code. Next they would swear the thirty-six time honoured oaths of loyalty. Each one would prick their middle finger and let the blood ooze into a cup, from which they all drank (still, Wang wondered, now this Western disease called AIDS was beginning to infect China?). The Incense Master, the lodge's expert on ritual, would teach the blue lanterns the society's codewords and recognition signals: the Shan Master would invite them to step across a symbolic river of burning paper—a one-way journey, according to Oath Thirteen. Finally, the neophytes would take meat cleavers to an effigy of Ma Ningyi, the renegade monk who had betrayed the first Triad group had betrayed the first Triad group, back in the era of the Manchu emperors.

In those far-off days, the Triads had been freedom fighters, eager to rid China of foreign invaders. They had changed slowly into criminals, especially once the last Manchu had been dethroned and they had no cause left to fight. Now they still talked the language of honour and patriotic rebellion—but the blue lanterns would have known exactly what sort of organization they were leaving their old lives to join.

Wang locked up his office and made his way down the stone steps of HQ into the main hall. The retired *Wujing* (SAS) sergeant on the front door wished him good night; Wang walked out into the smart concrete courtyard, then round to the rack at the rear of the building where his simple gearless black Phoenix bicycle stood waiting for him. (The motorbike was a departmental one, for work hours only: only when Wang was a team-leader would he have one that he could ride home.)

As he pulled out into the still-busy traffic of Qianmen East Street, Wang pondered what his next move should be. The author of that report, Inspector Liu—he must speak to the fellow tomorrow morning.

A traffic light went red, and Wang pulled up. He wondered what Chen, Zhao and the rest of the team were doing now, back at Huashan.

Nothing remotely as interesting as this, he told himself.

• • •

Wang put a call through first thing next morning.

"Can I speak to Inspector Liu Qiang?"

"No."

"Why not?"

"He's dead. Heart attack, three months ago."

Wang's eyes widened. "We need to talk. Are you busy?"

"We're always busy."

"I'm coming over now."

Inspector Liu's colleagues remembered him with little affection.

"He was a loner," said his team-leader. "And obsessive. I let him get on with his stuff as much as I could. He was very bitter—about lack of support for his ideas." He gave a shrug. "There was never enough money for the kind of in-depth investigation he wanted. He should have been born twenty years earlier: you know what it's like now, everything has to be costed."

Wang nodded his head in agreement.

"He didn't keep fit," the team-leader went on. "And he smoked. You've read the latest Party directive on smoking, of course?"

"Of course. Where did he die?"

"Here. He often used to work over lunch break—typical; the fellow lived for his job. One day, I came back and found him slumped over his desk."

"Any clues as to—"

"It was natural. Of course, we had a post-mortem, but there were no signs of any foul play. Most of us wondered why it hadn't happened earlier."

"So it was common knowledge, his heart condition?"

"Oh, yes. You'd only need to pass the poor old sod wheezing up the stairs. 'The day is waning and the road ending.' "

Wang nodded again. "Does he have any family?"

"No."

"None?"

"Not to our knowledge."

Such a thing would have been unheard of in Nanping village, where life was still dominated by family and clan. In the modern city . . .

"I guess we all feel guilty we weren't more friendly to him," the team-leader said suddenly. "But he wasn't the sociable type. We'd all go out for a meal sometimes—eat a bit, drink a bit. He never came with us."

"Did he leave anything else apart from his Triad file?"

The team-leader shook his head, but a sergeant began rummaging in a drawer.

"His diary," he said, holding out a small green book.

Liu Qiang's name was in the front, in correct, careful calligraphy. Then came a few appointments and a work schedule. January was to be dedicated to the Green Circle. A name was written at the top of one page: *Luo Pang.* From February onwards, there was nothing.

"When did Inspector Liu die?" Wang asked.

"12th January."

Wang returned to his own office, where he checked through the dead inspector's file for references to Luo Pang. There were none. So was this a new suspect: the Shan Master, perhaps? Or just another coded password? Or a false trail? For the moment there didn't seem to be any way of finding out.

Back to what Wang did know. Xun's links with Ren Hui— the Enforcer of the lodge, the man whose job it would be to punish any blue lantern who broke the sacred oaths. By death?

Colonel Da was seventy-five—almost old enough for the Politburo, as Zhao said when Team-leader Chen wasn't around. He had been on the Long March; he had fought the Japanese in Shanxi province, the Nationalists in Manchuria and the West in Korea. Now he sat in an office on the fifth floor where he appeared to spend all day drinking export-only tea and filling in forms.

Wang liked to think of the colonel as a friend rather than just a contact. Before joining the police, Wang had served in the People's Liberation Army. He had even won a medal— Combat Hero Second Class, during China's brief but bitter border war with its former ally, Vietnam. Wang had kept in touch with his old commanding officer on the Yunnan front; when the inspector was posted to the capital, Colonel Li had told him to contact Da. Wang had done so, and the two men had taken a liking to one another at once. Da was a fighter of the old school; his stories of revolutionary heroism and self-sacrifice fascinated Wang. Da, in turn, respected Wang for his medal and because the inspector had a reputation for integrity—not to mention the capacity to sit and listen to stories. Wang asked as few favours from the colonel as he could, and when he did, they were of a professional, rather than a personal, nature. Like today.

"It's the only way forward," he explained. "I must have a close look at this fellow."

"It's risky," Da replied. He took the lid off his tea cup and sniffed the steam. "Another minute, I think."

"I'm aware of the risks, sir. Inspector Liu's file is full of background information on people like Enforcer Ren—even down to names of old friends from twenty years back. He obviously had an undercover operation in mind."

"Hmm. Internal Security aren't keen on CID personnel snooping around in plain clothes. They'll make a fuss . . ." The old man paused. "But I'll stand up for you. I don't like the way they meddle in departmental affairs—any more than you do." He sniffed the tea again.

"They . . ." On the floors below, people said that Da worked for Internal Security. The old man always denied it vigorously, but told Wang not to pass the denials on to anyone. "If they dislike me enough to gossip behind my back," Da argued, "it's best if they also fear me."

The old campaigner raised the mug to his lips and drank. "Perfect!"

Wang drank, too. The tea was delicious: top quality Dragon Well, its infusion timed to perfection.

"I'll need money," said Wang, after a long, savoured draught. Da produced a form from a drawer and began to fill it in, in youthful, vigorous characters.

"Maximum two thousand yuan. You know my feelings about fiddling expenses . . . Take this to Bu in Treasury tomorrow. Don't let Team-leader Chen see it; he's a stickler for protocol. Or that colleague of yours, Inspector Zhao; he's ambitious. And sharp."

Sometimes Wang wondered how Da knew so much about

what went on in the department. Those denials weren't false, were they? Nobody in the criminal police liked Internal Security; if Wang found out Da was *Ke Ge Bo* after all, he would feel profoundly betrayed. Profoundly. He watched the colonel finish the form. No, this was just an old man who had perfected the art or survival under the most difficult conditions possible . . .

"Here you are," said Da. He took another sip of tea. "Of course, I remember the first anti-Triad campaigns, back in the fifties . . ."

Wang glanced at his watch and sat back in his seat.

A hazy bloodshot sun was sinking behind the random jumble of gables, smokestacks, trees, power-lines, apartment blocks and TV aerials that was the Chongwen skyline. The air was heavy with pollution and the heat of an early spring day; the road was full of rush-hour noise—air-horns, bicycle-bells, crowds jostling along the bumpy concrete pavements. Somewhere, a traffic policeman blew a whistle. At whom? Nobody knew; nobody cared.

Wang, now in a Western suit, patted the briefcase on his knee and wound the taxi's electronic windows back up.

"Remember your name," he told Constable Lu.

"Yes, sir. It's Bo."

"Just down here, isn't it, sir?" said the driver, also a CID man.

"That's right." Wang glanced across at Lu again. Was his assistant the right companion for this mission? Lu would be good in a fight, but the best undercover agents never got into fights in the first place. But Wang needed company: two pairs of eyes were very much better than one. The CID was perpetually short of manpower: Wang was lucky to have an assistant at all.

The taxi pulled up by a teastall and the two passengers got out. Wang paid the driver then walked over to a man reading yesterday's *People's Daily*.

"Mr. Jin?" he asked: the man lowered his head and nodded . . .

The moment they left the main road, Wang and Lu re-entered the silent, unchanging world of courtyards and alleyways—the *hutongs* of Chongwen. These might have been designed for intrigue and covert assignments, so winding, uniform and complex were they. When the three men stopped outside a doorway guarded by two weather-beaten stone lions, Lu was totally lost.

"Pickaxe Alley," Wang told himself.

The guide rang a bell. Footsteps. The door opened a crack; the guide had a whispered conversation with someone, then beckoned them in. Down a corridor, through an arch into a tidy, well-kept yard. At the far end was a two-storey house with a façade of fresh stucco. Somewhere inside it, a woman was singing a wistful folk tune.

"How lovely," Wang muttered.

"What?" said Lu.

"The song."

"Oh, yes," Lu answered flatly: it reminded him of cultural evenings at pioneer camp, of boredom and guilt.

The man crossed to the stuccoed house and rapped four times on the door. Wang made a mental note of the rhythm. The man who answered was wearing a pinstripe suit, black and white leather brogues and a bright purple shirt with matching tie. Ren Hui, importer/exporter and Red Cudgel for the Green Circle lodge.

"Mr. Ling! Come in. And your colleague, too."

The visitors did so. The hall had thick pile carpet and imitation silk wallpaper. Pricey. The gangster closed the door and bolted it, top and bottom.

"So you knew my old friend Shi?"

"That's right," said Wang. "Back in Jinan days, of course. Times have changed a lot since then." The inspector held out his card.

LING WUDA. PROCUREMENT MANAGER, VICTORY ELECTRONICS FACTORY.

"Shi and I went in, er, different directions," Wang continued. How thorough chain-smoking, Triad-obsessed Inspector Liu had been! "But we've both moved on in the world."

Ren Hui laughed. "And now you're after air-conditioners, right?"

"Yes. Productivity tumbles the moment summer comes. You know what it's like."

"Not really." Ren flicked a switch and a jet of cold air swirled past Wang's head. "Come through."

The sitting room was even more luxurious. A huge television dominated one corner; best Xinjiang carpets overlapped one another on the floor; the walls were hung with tapestries. Opposite the window was a desk, on top of which sat a porcelain statuette of Buddha Maitreya. Ren noticed his visitor's interest in this latter and nodded.

"Southern Song dynasty."

"It's lovely," Wang said. Even the stuff vanishing from Huashan was crude compared to this: the Southern Song was the high-point of Chinese Buddhist sculpture. If the piece was genuine, it was worth more than an honest worker would earn in his lifetime.

"Drink, gentlemen?" Ren crossed to a lacquer cupboard—another antique—and opened it. The inside had been gutted and turned into storage space for bottles of foreign spirits. Wang reined in his disgust and asked for a beer. Chinese, if possible.

Ren called out: "Yujiao!" The singing stopped and a young woman entered from a side door. She was tall and slim, graceful and confident; she wore a shiny emerald *qipao* dress with a side-slit way beyond her knee; her face was made up to look assertively Western.

"Very fashionable," Wang said to himself with more than a hint of disapproval. Then she turned to him and gave a delicate, totally Chinese smile, and his disapproval melted. Those eyes, so like Mei's . . .

"These gentlemen want some Chinese beer," Ren said, putting a subtle sneer into the last two words—what hicks these manufacturers could be, ordering Chinese stuff when there were foreign products on offer! "Do we have any in the house?"

"Yes, Father."

"What brand?"

"Beijing."

"Is that all right, Mr. Ling?"

"Excellent."

"Mr. Bo?"

Lu was silent.

"Bo?" said Wang. Hell, the stupid kid has forgotten his alias.

"Me? Oh, yes! That'll be great . . ."

Ren Yujiao went out, and came back with three dark brown bottles glistening on a mother-of-pearl tray. She began to pour.

"My daughter is the best singer in China," said Ren.

Yujiao blushed but said nothing.

"And the most beautiful," Ren continued.

She blushed even more.

Wang made a suitably polite comment, while an inner voice objected that she deserved more than this vulgar Western-style showing-off. Ren Yujiao handed the drinks round, then headed for the door.

"Stay and amuse us, Yujiao," Ren told her.

"I've work to do, Father." She smiled and left.

Ren shook his head. "She knows her own mind, that girl. And she's so talented. Singing, dancing, acting. She's got a great future." He raised his glass. *"Ganbei!"* Cheers!

"Ganbei!" the policemen replied, and drank. The singing began again, this time in a foreign language.

"Yesterday, all my troubles seemed so far away . . ."

"Now, this machinery you want to get hold of. It's not easy to come by. I'll need an advance."

"Of course." Wang reached for his wallet and produced two rolls of hundred-yuan Foreign Exchange Certificates. Ren Hui stuffed them casually into his pocket.

"The real money will come on sight of the goods," Wang added.

"Of course."

"Oh, I believe in yesterday . . ."

The gangster shook his head again. There was a look of genuine sadness in his eyes. "I wish she'd sing something a bit more cheerful."

And Chinese, Wang thought.

By the time the deal had been worked out in detail, a lot of alcohol had been consumed. Wang steered the conversation on to business contacts, then dropped the name Xun Yaochang into it. Ren Hui, who was halfway through a mouthful, nearly choked.

"You've dealt with him?" he asked, wiping the beer off his suit with a silk handkerchief.

"Only briefly. Was that unwise?"

"No. I don't really know the fellow. I've heard he's not very reliable, that's all. I wouldn't do business with him."

"I won't," said Wang. He didn't mention the name again; he didn't need to.

"So you reckon it's him?" said Lu, as the two men sat in the back of another taxi.

"We need to know more," Wang replied.

A lot more, Wang added to himself. If Xun Yaochang had broken the Triad code, why deal with him that way? Wheels Chai had spotted that at once. Inspector Liu's files were clear on the matter. Triad justice was meted out as ritualistically as Triad initiation. Were Xun a simple traitor, he should have received "death by ten thousand swords"—which nowadays usually meant five or six meat cleavers, wielded by Xun's fellow recruits under Ren Hui's supervision. There was more to this case than that. Unfortunately, today's outing hadn't revealed what.

Still, it was always interesting to meet the Enforcer of a Triad lodge.

"We are making progress," Wang told his team-leader as he tidied his files away. It was Friday: no work this afternoon. Political Study instead. Chen, Inspector Zhao and Sergeant Fang had returned from the Huashan site, in time to shower red dust off themselves and smarten up for the session, which was attended by everyone in the department. Everyone, that was, who wanted to get anywhere.

It was held in an auditorium with a stage and raised banks of seats. During the Cultural Revolution, this room had witnessed the humiliation of a number of the capital's finest police officers; since then it had been the venue for regular Political Study sessions and the occasional talk on criminology. Party Secretary Wei took the chair, as usual.

"Today is a particularly important session," the Secretary began, also as usual. "Now, I know the incidents on Tiananmen Square were nearly two years ago, but there are still, er, ramifications that have to be dealt with. Our leaders have decided to launch a new campaign: Strengthen the Party. I have details here.''

He glanced round at his audience. Usually people would have opened newspapers or files by now and would be covertly reading them. But not today, not after that announcement.

''It's quite simple. All Party members will make a thorough self-criticism of their thoughts and actions from 26th April to 4th June 1989. We will then formally resign our membership.'' He paused, to let his words sink in. ''Then, of course, we apply to rejoin. The point is that vetting procedures, which we normally apply to others, will be applied to ourselves. All of us.'' The Party Secretary grinned. ''This is not a witchhunt. We have no quotas of rightists to fill. The aim is to increase our self-awareness, to see how we made mistakes, to prevent such mistakes happening again. I feel we should be glad of the opportunity the Party is offering us. A chance to close the door and think carefully. A chance to improve ourselves, to follow the example of Comrade Lei Feng . . .''

Inspector Zhao grimaced. Lei Feng was a revolutionary soldier who always volunteered for extra work: since his death, Lei had been the subject of endless emulation campaigns. Even good Party members—and Zhao made sure he was one of the best—were getting fed up with him.

''Honesty is the keyword Secretary Wei continued. He looked round at his men. ''Comrade Wang, you don't agree?''

''No. I mean, yes, of course I do . . .''

Saturday night. Late. Wang was still at his desk. He made himself another cup of green tea, scratched his head, glanced up at his calligraphy-scroll—JUSTICE—then returned his attention to the piece of paper in front of him.

''My name is Wang Anzhuang. I am an inspector in the Criminal Investigation Department of the Beijing Public Security Bureau. This is a detailed account of my thoughts and actions from 26th April to 5th June 1989 . . .''

This was a moment Wang had been dreading.

4

May 1989. The Beijing Spring.

Initially, Wang had been hostile to the protesting students—how dare a small, pampered elite carry on this way, jamming up the capital, talking down to top Party leaders, making China lose face in front of the whole world? The inspector had even volunteered for extra duty, to go out on to the streets and help the regular city police keep order. He'd been set to guard the census office, outside which a small group of protestors had encamped. They seemed eager to talk with anyone; Wang was soon drawn into arguments.

"You should realize what the Party has achieved since liberation," he told them, quoting facts and figures—infant mortality, literacy rates, GNP levels. "For example, in 1949 the life-expectancy of the average Chinese was below forty; now it's seventy. Think of all those extra years."

They, in turn, compared China with Taiwan, Japan, Hong Kong and America. And they claimed to be patriots, too: "We're not just doing this for ourselves. It's for China. We love our country; we want it to be as good as these places."

"It will be. But you must give the reforms time."

"How much time? We do not want to end our lives with China still backward."

"You won't. Why should you?"

"Because of corruption, because of nepotism, because of endless cover-ups of official incompetence. Only democracy will stop these things."

Wang disliked their parroting of this Western word. Did they know what it meant? No two of them seemed to have the same definition . . . But another side of him knew that the protestors had a point. There were things wrong with the existing system. Their intentions were good. If only they'd tone down their objections, talk sensibly with the Party—negotiation and consensus, that was the Chinese way.

One day, a young woman came up to the inspector and offered him a flower. She had red cheeks, keen intelligent eyes and a gawky, peasant style of speech. That accent—she wasn't a city girl; was she from Shandong province, too? Listening to her speak, Wang saw Nanping village again, its one rutted mud street surrounded by thatched hovels; the brick Party offices where his father had sat struggling through paperwork; the Ancestral Hall, officially closed, but still secretly decked with flowers, food and hell-money the night before feast days like Qing Ming or Autumn Moon . . . He knew he should refuse the gift. He accepted it and took it home.

Another evening, the protestors wanted to light a fire. That was also against the rules—but Wang let them go ahead, anyway. It was worth it; he felt real pleasure watching the light glowing on their faces and listening to the music they made as they sat there. This, too, brought back memories—of Army training, of camp in Yunnan, of the company of fellow soldiers, honourable, brave and public-spirited. When they began to sing the *Internationale* he joined in.

But with summer came heat, anger and brinkmanship. Troublemakers had infiltrated the student ranks—people Wang later saw in official videos attacking Army vehicles with clubs and petrol bombs. He warned his students about them; their response was naïve—they didn't want to be elitist and turn help away. He wrote a memorandum to his superiors, advising them to distinguish carefully between serious protestors and disruptive elements. Luckily for him, the memo had got lost somewhere.

On 1st June, he was moved to Muxudi, a strategic road junction a couple of miles west of Tiananmen Square. The

Army was closing in on the capital now, and a call went up
for the townspeople to defend the students. Tens of thousands
responded. Soldiers were sent in to disperse them—unarmed
peasant boy recruits in trainers and casual clothes. The Beijingers stood and argued with them; the lads listened, then retreated in confusion. Wang watched them go with mixed
feelings. Something had to be done to bring the capital back
to normal: making the People's Liberation Army look foolish
was not that something. But what was?

Next evening the crowds were out again, and a new force
was sent in, uniformed and armed. Wang recognized them at
once as the Twenty-seventh Division, a crack unit based in
Shijiazhuang. They lined up and fired their AK47s into the
air. The crowd began to disperse. Wang watched with ap-
proval. Well done, boys—a nicely balanced show of power.
Show them who's boss, but nobody gets hurt.

Then suddenly the rifle barrels lowered. An order was
shouted, and the men began pumping bullets into the retreating
Beijingers. The People's Liberation Army was firing on the
people.

Wang couldn't believe it. "Stop!" he found himself shouting. "There must be a mistake! They have no weapons!"

Nobody heard above the moans of the dying and the rattle
of the Kalashnikovs. He began to run towards the soldiers.

"I demand to see your commanding officer! Stop shooting
at once!" Then a bullet hit him in the leg, and he fell to the
ground. People were running all round him, screaming, in
panic. Pure self-preservation took over and Wang began to
hobble back with them. A nineteen-year-old girl pitched forward on to her face in front of him: he tried to pick her up,
but the pressure of fleeing Beijingers drove him by. Glancing
back, seeing the blood pumping out of a great hole between
her shoulders, there wouldn't have been any point, anyway.
In a terrible second of absolute fury, Wang thought the un-
thinkable, that if he had a rifle of his own, he would stand up
and use it against his own beloved PLA . . .

Two days later, of course, the same troops went into Tiananmen Square. A clampdown followed: luckily Wang had
enough criminal work to be too involved. Now, two years on,

things were dying down. But someone wanted them stirred up again. What should Wang do?

"The gun shoots the bird that sticks its head up," an inner voice whispered. It had a strong Shandong accent; it belonged to his grandmother, Peng. "If you learn one thing, it should be that everything changes with time. *Yang* gives way to *Yin*."

Yes. He had kept his head well down as an Army recruit during the madness of the Cultural Revolution and survived. He had prevaricated since June '89 and life had returned to normal. He could weather this storm, too . . . But was that what he wanted?

He glanced up at his scroll again. People like his father and Colonel Da had risked their lives for their beliefs. Twelve years ago, he had done the same in a battle for a palm-topped hill on the Vietnam border. Was he now to spend the rest of his life head down, never fighting for anything except his own survival and convenience?

The thought disgusted him. But what was the alternative?

Constable Lu didn't sleep at all on Saturday night. And precious little on Sunday. On Monday morning, he got up at first light and took the longest cold shower of his life. As he dressed, he checked his clothing—a recent article in *Socialist Youth* had said that this sort of thing could be caused by tight-fitting underpants. But they were as baggy as ever.

"Spiritual Pollution, that's what it is," he muttered, and felt revolted at himself.

Yet as he took his bike out of the rack, he wished the old man from Flat 1406 a healthy "Good morning!" And as he pedalled into town past the bright concrete towers of the Asian Games Village and the ancient wooden gate of the Temple of the Earth, he found himself weaving in and out of the other riders as if he were winning a race. The sun was shining; the neat rows of plane trees beside the cycle lane were bursting into leaf—this thing called spring seemed to have more power than even ideology or love of country. As such, he knew he should be wary of it—but suddenly he couldn't bring himself to be so.

BE MORAL! a hoarding adjured him.

Yes, of course . . . Those thoughts that had buzzed around

his head all weekend were totally unworthy. He should be thoroughly ashamed of himself. Perhaps he should include a passage on the subject in his self-criticism. As he locked his bike into its rack, he hid his face from Mrs. Li, the old lady who watched over the rack during working hours. If she could read his mind, what would this fine veteran revolutionary say?

He found Wang already at work.

"Morning, sir!"

The inspector looked up. His face looked worn as if he too had spent a weekend in turmoil. In love, at his age? No, he must simply have been working extra hard.

"Found anything interesting, sir?"

"Not really. These other files just duplicate some of what Inspector Liu found out."

Lu looked disappointed.

"Our undercover operation was a success," Wang went on, forcing optimism into his voice. "But we need another line of approach, too."

Lu nodded his head, then an idea struck him. "What about his daughter? Have you looked to see if there's anything on file about her? There might be some leads."

"Hmm. Hadn't thought of that."

"I could do some investigating if you like."

"Yes, well, why not? I believe she sings under the stage name Jasmine. At the Qianlong Hotel, one of these big Western places. There'll be a file on the hotel; you could start there. And then . . ." the inspector's voice trailed away. "She's an attractive young woman, isn't she?"

Lu blushed. "Well, yes, sir."

"Not the sort of girl you meet at pioneer camp."

"No, sir. But I'm sure—with a bit of re-education . . ."

"Maybe she doesn't want re-education."

Lu looked puzzled.

"Her father's a gangster. From what I can gather, a ruthless—"

"That's not her fault!" Lu exclaimed. "If bourgeois influences persist in our society—"

"You stick to your work. Let the Party sort out the bourgeois influences." Wang looked sternly at the young man, then felt a pang of guilt. It *was* a good idea, checking up on

Ren Yujiao. He should have thought of it himself. Maybe if she hadn't reminded him of Mei, his ex-wife, he would have done. "OK. If you think it's worthwhile building up a dossier on Miss Ren, then go ahead. But keep a low profile. Low. Got it?"

"Yes, sir."

Lu picked up a file and strode purposefully out of the office. Wang wondered if he was doing the right thing. But he was always complaining that too much initiative was stifled in the force. Good to give the lad a chance.

Wang spent the day at the People's Theatre, interviewing vendors in the *hutong* outside, showing them a photo of Xun Yaochang and asking: "Have you seen this man?" Only the photographer thought he had. Xun had posed for a cheap, instant portrait. When? Some time ago. Not 15th April? Oh, no, a long time before that. Alone? No, he had a woman with him. Nervous type. Camera-shy.

The photographer took the police mug shot of Xun and stared at it. "Not a very good picture, is it?" he said. "I'm surprised at the People's Police using such outdated equipment. My stuff is the latest. Here's a card."

In the evening, Wang and Sergeant Ye gave handbills to all the opera-goers, asking if they had been at the performance last week and offering a cash reward for information leading to the arrest of a wanted murderer. Everyone suddenly remembered Xun—a hundred different Xuns.

One witness alone seemed to be telling the truth, an old man in a battered Western suit. "He was sitting in the back row. Dead drunk."

"Who was next to him?"

"Someone. I didn't notice them, though."

"Think. The person next to him."

The witness scratched his head. "Someone in grey?"

"Grey. You're sure?"

"I think so."

"Anything else you can tell us about him?"

"No." The witness paused. "Oh, yes. He had dark glasses on. All the young men seem to do that nowadays. 'Words can lie, the eyes image the soul.'"

Wang smiled—a quote from Mencius: what a splendid, scholarly old fellow!

"Do I get my money?" said the witness.

Constable Lu wheeled his bike up to the perimeter wall of the Qianlong Hotel and cast a quick glance over his shoulder. No one was looking. He hid the machine in a thorn bush and made his way on foot to the main gate.

"I can't do any harm," he said to himself. A jackdaw screeched; Lu's heart leapt, then he took some of those deep breaths Wang had taught him. Keep cool. This was going to be a combination of business and pleasure. Maybe he'd find some important clue—in a particularly absurd flight of fancy, he imagined himself sitting right behind Ren Hui and overhearing the guy say how he'd murdered this traitor at the opera. Would he arrest Ren there and then, or wait to tell the inspector next day?

The pleasure element of the evening was obvious.

At the bottom of the hotel drive was a guardpost. The occupant, whose job it was to keep Chinese out of this exclusive foreigners-only establishment, glared at the young man striding towards his window.

"What d'you want?"

"CID," replied the young man, producing his identity card with a flourish.

"So?"

"Special mission," said Lu.

"Crap!"

"I . . . It's very . . . Now, wait a minute—"

The guard began laughing. "Shall I phone your HQ to check?"

"No. I've said, it's a special mission."

More laughter.

"What are you after? Export-only goods from the Friendship Store? Kick-back on the new pool contract? Or just a bit of bourgeois decadence up there in the Starlight Suite?"

Lu was dumbstruck.

"Oh, go on," said the guard. "If anyone asks, you climbed over the wall, OK?"

Lu grinned and walked off as fast as dignity would allow.

The gateman returned to his magazine—*Shanghai Movie Pictorial* on the outside, a Hong Kong soft porn mag on the inside—shaking his head and muttering about the age of policemen nowadays.

Jasmine Ren walked out on to the stage to the usual burst of applause. From the side of the stage, Eddie Zheng grinned gormlessly up at her. The young floor manager's infatuation was as total and pathetic as ever. Who else was here? The spotlights didn't allow the singer to see too far into the audience, but Ken Wakamatu and Ray Schrader were both at their usual, front tables. Alone with candles, ice buckets and champagne—French, of course, not that cheap, sweet Russian stuff. She awarded both businessmen a smile before beginning her act.

"Welcome to the Starlight Suite," she said in English, Japanese and, in case there was anyone here from Taiwan, Mandarin. "I'm Jasmine, and I'm here to sing for you. Later on, it will be your turn to sing for me!" She turned and grinned at Ken, whose karaoke version of *My Way* never failed to reduce the band to laughter.

"I'd like to begin this evening with a song from America," (time for Ray to get a special look). "*Black Velvet* by Alannah Myles."

More applause. The bass began playing a C, in a slow, heartbeat pulse; drums joined in on kick-pedal and backbeat; the bassman played that gorgeous fill (listen to the original). Then Jasmine put her lips to the mike and let out a kind of anguished, ecstatic moan that made even the barman stop and stare out at the stage. Madame Mao, who had died a few months back, was surely turning in her grave.

After verse two, the guitar took a lead. Another chance for Jasmine to scan the audience . . . Both Ken and Ray had expressed their admiration for her with compliments and presents. Both wanted to become her lover. Jasmine wasn't interested; she didn't fancy them; she didn't have to take what she didn't want. And she knew how Daddy would feel if she slept with a foreigner. At the end of the number, the two businessmen tried to outdo each other in their applause. She thanked them with more flashing smiles. No harm in flirting, of course.

Outside, Lu walked up to the doorman and tried his ID again.

"Have you got a ticket, Comrade?" the doorman asked.

"No. Look!"

"I can read. But there's no crime going on in there. Entry for non-residents is twenty-five yuan in Foreign Exchange Certificates."

"Twenty-five . . ."

"Or ten dollars US."

"Ten dollars! May I remind you that the People's Police have a right to—"

"This particular People's Policeman is trying to get into a very popular show without paying."

"This is part of a criminal investigation."

"D'you want a word with the manager?"

"No . . ." said Lu despondently. From behind the doors, a voice began to sing: "*Yesterday, all my troubles seemed so far away.*" The young man's whole inside seemed to tighten. The doorman noticed his expression and either felt pity or the opportunity for a special deal.

"Have you got ten yuan?"

"Only *renminbi*," Lu replied—the currency that ordinary Chinese citizens use.

"Give it to me." The man took the grubby note and stuffed it into his wallet. "And don't try and bullshit me again. Welcome to Capitalism!"

"Thanks." That word was abhorrent to Lu: Capitalism meant selfishness, greed, disloyalty, immorality. But now it also meant hearing and seeing Jasmine's show. He slipped in through the door and joined his fellow-sinners.

The first set was drawing to a close. Jasmine looked round at the audience again. She began to speak; Eddie Zheng tore himself away to put up the house lights.

"We'll be back again soon with some more music from around the world—this time, with your help."

Ken grinned; he'd been practising. Jasmine lingered on stage to smile back. The lights went up. She lingered even

longer. It wasn't just Ken and Ray staring up at her but the
whole world. A big, rich world—men in thousand-dollar suits;
women in dresses that cost years' wages for a Chinese. The
one mainlander there—a young guy at the back, quite hand-
some and thoroughly embarrassed—stood out a mile.

There was something familiar about him.

"Come on, Jasmine. Off the stage," the bandleader hissed.
"It's unprofessional."

She obeyed, suddenly strangely ill-at-ease. Where had she
seen the young Chinese's face before?

"Who cares?" She retreated into her dressing room. "He's
just someone who's seen me around town, and who's found
a back door into one of my shows." But she felt no better.
The Starlight Suite was a charmed circle of opulence and
glamour. Beijing, dirty, tough and poor, stood outside that circle; whenever it tried to break in, she felt threatened.

"I must find out who he is," she told herself.

5

The whole of the next day was a nightmare of indecision for Constable Lu. Should he tell the inspector about last night, or keep silent and hope that nothing had really meant what he feared? As the young policeman pedalled home past the turreted walls of the Forbidden City, that incident replayed itself in his mind for the ten thousandth time that day—Jasmine up there on the stage; the house lights flashing on; her gaze, straight at him; her look of recognition and the shock that had gone with it. Then the questions. Supposing she asks around to find out who I am? Supposing she talks to the doorman, or the gatekeepers . . .

The same inner voice that had kept him going all day argued back confidently: *Why should she ask around? I wasn't in uniform. She just thinks I'm a young businessman. People like that are always bribing their way into the Qianlong.*

But the way she kept glancing my way in the second set . . . And if she does investigate, she'll find out who I really am!

He had resolved to tell Wang that morning. But the opportunity hadn't arisen. His boss had been down at the theatre again. Then Team-leader Chen had rung up from Huashan with some instructions about filing which had kept him in the library all afternoon. Afterwards, he'd sat in the office for a whole extra hour, waiting in vain for Wang to return.

He stopped at a market a few streets from home and wandered down the stalls. Perhaps, in the noise and bustle, he could lose himself. He bought an ice-cream and a comic—*Debt of Honour*. It was about the Vietnam war and this secret mission to blow up a Viet ammunition dump. Somebody gives the secret away . . .

Lu threw it in a bin and pedalled home. Mum and Dad were still at work—Trade Ministry officials work as long hours as policemen—so he sat down in front of the TV and put on a Martial Arts video. *Revenge of the Lost Warriors*. In the original, the Warriors had been unwittingly betrayed by one of their number.

He had to do something. To make sure. For himself.

Wang had a fruitless day interviewing shopkeepers in and around Dazhalan. Yes, they sold pocket knives. Two weeks ago? They couldn't remember. None of them recognized a picture of Ren Hui. The inspector returned to the office, arriving a few minutes after Lu had left, and spent a while rereading Inspector Liu's Triad file.

Justice in the Willow City is always enforced with maximum violence, Wang read—he was getting used to the terminology now: the Willow City, a term he associated with the Buddhist heaven, was for a Triad "hero" the lodge, all-encompassing and impossible to leave.

Maximum violence? Xun had been killed subtly. Yet the look on Ren's face when Wang had mentioned Xun . . .

He glanced up at the clock. Time to go home again. And to forget work for one evening. Forget, OK?

Wang rode home through the diesel fumes and racket. Forget. He would cook a meal; he would do some *qigong* exercises. He would read—the new edition of *October*, the short story magazine, had just arrived; if the censors had got at it, he would go back to the classics. *Sun Tzu's Art of War. The Water Margin. The Romance of the Three Kingdoms.* Or something more exotic, another one of those tales from that bizarre, far-off place called England: *The Adventures of Sherlock Holmes*.

Wang's near neighbour Mrs. Zeng was emptying a dustbin

as he coasted into the compound of Tiantan Inner Eastern
Building Twenty-six—a new, twelve-storey concrete block of
flats. She smiled at the inspector.

"Don't forget that dinner invitation," she said: the Zengs
had been very kind since the business with Mei.

Wang pushed his bike into the rack and flicked its rearwheel
lock shut. "I won't. Work hours are so irregular at the moment. When this case is over . . ."

"You'll be on another one."

Wang grinned. "You're right. We'll fix a day. Next month.
I won't be so busy then."

He took the creaking lift up to the tenth floor, and made his
way along the balcony past the strange assortment of objects
that even Party members end up storing outside their doors
due to lack of space. Flat 1008: home.

By Chinese standards, Wang's apartment was enormous.
Four rooms, just for one man! A sitting room at least ten feet
square. A bedroom almost as large, its walls lined with books.
A small kitchen and a stone-floored lavatory-cum-shower (hot
water twice a day, morning and evening). Flat 1008 had, of
course, once housed three people, but with Mei and Zhengyi
gone . . .

The inspector sat down on the one easy chair and found
himself staring at the photos on the heavy mahogany dresser.
In one frame, three army sergeants shared a packet of Double
Nine cigarettes and a joke, against an out-of-focus Vietnamese
jungle. Wan and Yi had both stopped bullets in the same action that Wang won his medal; Wan fatally, Yi invalided to a
desk for the rest of his life. Next to it was a family group:
granny Peng, his father and mother, brother Anming, sister
Chun, all dressed for 1st October celebrations in the late 'fifties. Then another family: Wang in police uniform, his wife
in a bright silvery dress from a Friendship Store, Wang Zhengyi in his young pioneer's white shirt and red scarf.

The old anger began to rise up again. Wang felt his nails
dig into the arms of the chair. Dammit, she'd known I'd
wanted to transfer to the police; she'd known what that would
mean in terms of time shared. And she'd known I wouldn't
use my job to get rich.

"You said you respected me for that," Wang muttered.

Then you started comparing me with other men: back-stabbers,
sellers of pardons, experts at fiddling expenses . . .

Wang sighed. All the blame on one side? Mei had wanted
more out of life than a man of Wang's background could offer;
he had played along, because he'd thought she would make
him urban and sophisticated, too. Looking back, he hadn't
even wanted to be like that. Not really, not deep down. He'd
cheated her; he'd cheated himself.

Divorce is such a messy business—so much shame; everybody knows, everyone gets involved. To help out, officially.
Or to gloat. And then there's Zhengyi . . .

Don't brood. Do something.

Wang enjoyed cooking as much as eating. He set some rice
up to boil then prepared some pork, cutting the salty outer
skin into cubes, searing them in oil and ginger then cooking
them in rice wine, soy, salt and sugar. When these were nearly
ready, he took off the rice, turned the power up to full and
stir-fried some Chinese beans. A feast, all done on two rings
of a burn-blackened mini-hob. He poured himself a glass of
beer and ate slowly, savouring the tastes he had inveigled into
the apparently simple ingredients. A bowl of stock soup followed, then a mug of tea.

Work? It was forgotten.

Qigong. First, a little stillness. Just sit and concentrate on
your own breath. In, out . . .

Wang had only had the phone fitted recently: its bell, ring-
ing right by his ear, made him jump with fright. He grabbed
the receiver.

"Who's that?"

Silence. Then a feeble, frightened voice. "It's me, Lu."

"Oh." Wang composed himself. "What's up?"

"I must talk to you. I wanted to wait, 'till the morning—
but, well, I can't."

"OK. I'm listening."

There was a sigh. "We couldn't meet, could we? I mean, I
don't trust the phone. People might be listening."

Wang gave a frown of puzzlement. "Well, if it's that important . . ." He paused to remind himself of where Lu lived.
"Meet me at Zhengyang Gate in half an hour."

A wistful glance at that copy of *October*. Mei had a point; who *would* marry a policeman?

Wang stood by the old gate and lit a cigarette. Starlings twittered in the rafters; soft music was playing from a nearby loudspeaker. In front of him was Tiananmen Square, that enormous concrete plain in the middle of the capital. Its dim ornamental lamps—eight-armed like Nezha, the capital's legendary founder—hewed dull pools of light out of its huge darkness. Around its sides, floodlights added a few features: the national emblem on the Great Hall of the People, the portrait of Mao on Tiananmen Gate, the flag on the Bank of China. The grand boulevards that ran up and down the sides were empty, apart from a few unlit bicycles and a policeman on a noiseless Japanese motorbike—yet the Square wasn't silent. Families had come out to stroll and chat. Two children were playing football, shrieking with happiness. A young couple walked hand in hand. The inspector took a drag at his Panda. What happened here two years ago was already history; life goes on.

"Wang!"

Constable Lu came into view. The young man looked terrible.

"What's up?" Wang asked.

"Nothing."

"Nothing?"

"I—I couldn't talk about it over the phone. Thanks for coming, sir—" Lu's voice died and his eyes fell to the ground.

"What on earth is it?"

"Well, sir, you know you told me to build up a dossier on Ren's daughter. Well, I was doing that, and . . . She's disappeared."

"Disappeared?"

"Last night I went to that hotel where she sings. To try and—"

"You did *what*?"

"I went to that hotel, the Qianlong, and . . ." Lu's voice died again. "I wasn't going to talk to anyone there, sir—just watch."

Wang opened his mouth to speak, then stuffed his cigarette into it and took a long, deep drag.

"That wasn't quite what I had in mind when I said low profile," he said ultimately.

"No, sir."

"Well, tell me what happened, anyway."

"I went to the back. Trying to look insignificant—"

"Was there another Chinese person in the room?"

"Well, no, sir, but . . . It would have been fine, but when the interval came, the lights went up. I—I think she saw me. She certainly looked in my direction."

"She recognized you?"

"I don't know. Yes, I think she might have done."

"Why didn't you tell me this today?"

Lu spread his arms. "You weren't around. I—"

Wang felt a rush of anger for the second time that evening. He fought it back: it doesn't do any good. "Never mind. What's all this about her disappearing, then?"

"Well, I went back there again this evening. To check, you see. I had to find out."

"*Ai-ya!* What are you trying to do? Why not write out a big character poster and pin it on the hotel wall?"

"I'm sorry, sir."

Wang looked away, sucked the last smoke out of his Panda then ground it into the concrete with his heel.

"OK. You went back again. What happened?"

"There wasn't a show. It had been cancelled. I asked why, and the doorman said Jasmine had reported sick."

"So? People do get sick. Even the young and beautiful."

Lu blushed. "It—just seemed a coincidence."

"Yes. You're right." Wang was always telling the young man that he didn't believe in coincidences. "This doorman. Did he know you were a policeman?"

"Yes, sir."

"Did you get the impression that he thought that fact was important? In other words, did he suspect a link between your snooping about and Ren Yujiao's sudden disappearance?"

"I'm not sure, sir. No, not really."

"And who else did you play the 'let me in, I'm Public Security' stunt on?"

Lu stared shamefully at the ground. "The gatekeeper, sir."

"Nobody else?"

"No."

"That's something, I suppose . . ."

A truck backfired on Qianmen West Street, sending the starlings whirling out across the night sky. Wang battled with his emotions.

"You were brave to come and tell me now, Lu," he said after a long pause. "Well done. We must move fast!"

Monkey-face Meng's fourth-floor door was plywood: when Wang knocked and no one answered, he told Lu to kick it down. The constable leant back and brought his boot down just behind the lock. The door splintered and yawned open; the two officers burst into a dingy bedsit. Wang's heart sank as he contemplated the clothes on the floor and the disarrayed bed.

"Too late!" Wang felt the anger at his young colleague rising again—but with it a callous excitement: at least this showed they were on the right track.

A head peeped up from behind the bed.

"Oh. It's you," it said.

"Yes. Why didn't you answer when we knocked."

"I was busy," said Meng. He stood up, draping a sheet around his naked body. "You've damaged my door."

"We'll send a man to repair it. If we'd have been the Yi Guan Dao, it would be more than your door that got broken."

That look of instant terror again. "They've found out what I told you?"

"No. But there's been, well, a hitch in our surveillance operation. I'm not taking any risks. So get dressed and packed."

"Where are you taking me?"

"Somewhere where you'll be safe."

"Jail? Just because you dogs can't keep a secret?"

"Because I keep my word. It's no problem for the department if you get beaten to pulp by Ren Hui and his friends. But I've got a conscience."

Meng looked at Wang suspiciously: he distrusted all policemen, especially when they started talking about conscience. But he feared the Yi Guan Dao.

"OK . . ." He began to gather his things: some clothes, a Walkman, the Taiwanese soft porn magazine over which he had been masturbating when the intruders arrived. Wang snatched the magazine and aimed to chuck it in the bin—then handed it back. Meng had had enough trouble for one evening.

Giddy from the lift ride, Wang stepped out on to the twentieth floor of the Qianlong Hotel. He padded across the thick crimson carpet to the doors of the Starlight Suite. They were open; he went in. There was a bar by the door, tables and chairs in the middle and a stage at the far end, crammed with the impedimenta of Western pop: drums, electric keyboards, amplifiers and microphone stands. A middle-aged woman was polishing the bar-rail: she glanced up at the new arrival, scowled and got back to work.

Wang made his way between the tables to the stage and hopped up on to it. Constable Lu said he had been standing in the far left-hand corner. About where the cleaner was now. Ren Yujiao could have recognized him easily.

Backstage was a tatty dressing room, along whose near wall were coat racks with sequinned costumes on rusty wire hangers and some mirrors with light sockets above them, mostly empty. A door led into a smaller room that was carpeted, well-lit and sweet-smelling. Two bouquets of flowers sat in vases: Wang bent down and read the labels. One in English, the other in Japanese.

That tingle at the back of his neck. Policeman's instinct: he was being watched. He turned to find a burly man with a scar on his chin standing in the outer doorway.

"Can I help?" said the man aggressively.

Don't be drawn in.

Wang smiled back. "I don't know. Are you part of the band?"

"No."

"Ah. I hear they put on a good show."

"They do. Very good. What's it to you?"

"I was wondering . . . I've always wanted to hear Western music. Is there any way you could get me a ticket?"

The man sneered. "You'd better speak to Mr. Zheng."

"And his office is . . . ?"

"Down the corridor, third right."

"Thanks," said Wang. He took one more look round the room, just to show the big man that he would leave in his own time—then left.

The young man with thick, fishbowl glasses grinned nervously as "Inspector Gao" introduced himself.

"I'm Eddie," he said in reply, pointing at a plastic badge on his lapel which said: HELLO—I'M EDDIE. CAN I HELP YOU?

"And your Chinese name?" said Wang.

"Kangmei. Zheng Kangmei."

Wang nodded: even he had to admit that Kangmei—Resist America!—wasn't the ideal name for someone showing the Qianlong's guests to their 400-dollar-a-night suites.

"How can I help you, Inspector?"

"I've heard good things about the show here."

Eddie smiled. "Jasmine is the most talented singer we've had in this place. Ever. We've been packing people in for the last few months. Of course I knew straight away. At the audition—her first number. D'you know that song *Feelings*, by Morris Albert?"

Wang shook his head.

"The moment I heard it, I said we've got to have her . . . It wasn't easy, though. She's a good negotiator. Tough—on the outside anyway. Inside . . . Ah, but how can I help?"

"I'd like to come and see her show."

"Ah. When she comes back . . ."

"She's taking a break?"

"No." The young man paused. "Actually, seeing as you're a policeman. I was wondering . . ." He stared down at the desk. "I know it sounds silly, but, well, she didn't turn up for work last night. Nothing odd in that, you might say—but she's never done that before. Never. She's a real professional. I've seen her knocked out with flu, and still go up on stage and give a wonderful performance. Wonderful. And when she went through all this business with that dreadful boyfriend . . . But last night it was a simple call, in the midafternoon, 'I can't make it this evening. Sorry.' Nothing else. That's not like her, Inspector. Not at all."

Wang nodded. "My business is chasing up forged bank-notes. But if she doesn't appear in the next couple of days, give me a call. I can make some discreet inquiries." He wrote a number and a name down on a piece of paper.

Eddie was instantly happy again. "It's been awful these last twenty-four hours, I can tell you. What'll we do without her?" He began to tell the inspector about Jasmine's skill, natural-ness, toughness, vulnerability, charisma, humanity, determi-nation, warm-heartedness (and so on): Wang listened patiently till five-to, when he tapped his watch and said he had to be going.

"Remember to get in touch," he said as he left.

"I shall."

Wang and Lu walked into the team office. It was empty: as Chen's assistant, Tan, had just been sent to collect a file, it would stay that way for at least ten minutes.

"There's something odd about that hotel," Wang explained. "I need to talk to the ISB man there." Internal Security have covert units watching all the major tourist hotels. "There'll be a code for contacting them—I wonder where Chen keeps the list?"

"Couldn't we ask switchboard, sir?"

"We could, but I think it's time you learnt some undercover skills." Wang glanced at the team-leader's desk. "Fetch me a length of wire."

"Wire, sir?"

"Wire, Lu."

Lu went into the inspector's office, rummaged through a drawer and came back with a piece. It was too thick; Wang went and got one himself.

"Note the size. Neither too thin nor too fat; too stiff nor too flexible."

Lu looked on in horror as his boss knelt down and broke into *his* boss's desk. And even more horror as Wang slammed it shut again and held the wire out.

"If you want to do any kind of undercover work, expertise with locks is essential. You only get good by practice. Your turn."

6

When Eddie Zheng rang, Lu took the call.

"Inspector Gao? I think you've got the wrong—oh, that Inspector Gao. You must be Eddie." He wasn't supposed to say that, either. Never mind: the guy was jabbering into the phone, he probably hadn't even noticed the slip-ups.

"Right, I'll tell him," said Lu, once a break came. "Four o'clock. At the Pearl Tea House. He'll be there, don't worry . . . Forgeries? What forg—oh, those forgeries. We are making excellent progress!"

The Pearl was a small café in the back alleys south of the Qianlong, run by an ex-policeman called Han. It had a corrugated iron roof and a front of dusty glass and unpainted wood; inside were an assortment of formica-topped tables and plastic fold-up chairs. The walls had been decorated with brightly-coloured posters of anything and everything Chinese: the Great Wall, the romantic pop-singer Deng Lijun, the three star gods of wealth, longevity and happiness, the great thirty-fifth anniversary parade in Tiananmen Square. At lunch time it was full of garrulous customers, an even more garrulous radio playing distorted Hong Kong disco, and smells of garlic, cigarettes, cooking oil, onion, soy and best *Zhenjiang* vinegar.

At three o'clock, it was empty and quiet.

Han put up the "closed" sign and went into the yard behind

to finish the washing-up. At five-to four, he reappeared and took the sign down. The young man with big glasses who had been loitering outside came in at once: an older man rode up on a bicycle a few minutes later and joined him. Once both customers were seated, Han closed shop again and went back to the kitchen. The less he overheard, the happier he was.

Eddie Zheng had bags under his eyes. As he picked up the stained brown menu, his hand shook.

"So you've heard nothing?" said Wang.

"Nothing. The manager has told me to book a stand-in. Who can I get to replace her?"

Wang shrugged. "The People's Liberation Army choir have some excellent soloists."

"You must get her back, Inspector. I'm sure something has gone wrong."

"You don't think she's got a better offer from another venue?"

"She was becoming the toast of the capital in the Starlight!"

"Maybe she's gone abroad. It does happen."

"No. Jasmine was happy with us. And she was a good patriot. She had no wish to go abroad."

Han brought some tea. Wang waited for his to infuse, while the young man gulped his down almost at once.

"But she had admirers, didn't she?" Wang went on. "Rich foreigners, that might have lured her overseas."

Eddie blushed. "She was a very attractive woman. There was an American. And a Japanese. But she never, you know, did anything immoral with them. She wasn't that type."

"Are you sure?"

"Well, I—yes. I am sure. I got to know her well. She confided in me." Eddie beamed with pride. "She needed someone strong in her life. Strong spiritually, not the kind of toughs that used to chase after her."

"Are both these foreigners still resident at the hotel?"

"I think so. I can find out if you like."

"Let me know if they're not," said Wang. "Who else was significant in Ren Yujiao's life? Anyone: Chinese, Western."

"There was me."

"Of course."

Eddie fell silent. "And, well—there was this boyfriend. It didn't last, of course. He was a bastard. The way he treated her . . ."

"What was his name?"

"I don't know. She never said."

"Did you ever see him?"

"Oh, no. If I had done, I'd have given him what for!"

Wang glanced at the young man's slight physique, and wondered what would have happened had he tried.

"You must have known something about this fellow, though. Did he ever come to the show?"

"Not to my knowledge."

Wang nodded. "That's a little odd. Perhaps he didn't like music." Or perhaps he did like music—proper Chinese music. "D'you know when they first met?"

"No. They were already together when we took Jasmine on, and that was three months ago."

"And when did they split up?"

"26th February. I'll never forget it. She was in tears; she said she wanted to die; she had a kind of fainting fit five minutes before curtain-up. Then the show began, and she went on and gave a marvellous performance—even by her standards. Inspector, you should have been there!"

Wang bit back a comment about the shows being for foreigners only. "Tell me about any other people in Jasmine's life. Any female friends?"

"I never met any. I think she preferred male company. Women can be very envious."

"And the band?"

"Friends—but no more. They all, er, desired her, of course. I'm afraid most Western-style musicians have very low minds."

"That follows. Tell me about Jasmine's family. Her father for example."

Eddie glanced away and said nothing.

"This discussion is in confidence," said Wang. The bespectacled eyes found his again. They were afraid.

"If you want me to help, you must give me as much information as you can."

"Yes . . ." said Eddie. "But I never met him. I know he

had a lot of power over her. And he had a reputation as a violent man. I once declared my, er, feelings, for Jasmine. Next day, a colleague of his came around, and threatened to kill me if I so much as touched her. I tried to explain that real love needn't involve all that physical stuff—the fellow just snarled and repeated his threat.''

"But you never met this father? He never came to see her show, or to talk to any of your colleagues?"

"Not to my knowledge."

"And has he been in touch with anyone since Jasmine's disappearance?"

"No. Well, not me, anyway."

"Is there anyone else in your organization that he might have contacted?"

"No idea . . . I was her direct boss."

"You, Zheng Kangmei, were responsible for hiring her?"

"Me and Mr. Li. Martinez, the bandleader, had a say too. Of course, with Jasmine it was easy. The moment she started singing—"

"Who's Mr. Li?"

"Our Profile Manager."

The inspector looked baffled.

"He runs all the entertainment, decides on the decor of new rooms, what sort of items we sell in the hotel shop, that kind of thing."

"Ah." Wang sniffed the tea: it was about ready to drink. "Li doesn't have a scar on his chin, does he?"

"No," Eddie replied. "That's Chao."

"Ah. Who's Chao?"

"I don't know. He's a maintenance worker or something. He hangs around the suite a lot—I think he knows someone in the band."

"Martinez?"

"Maybe. I don't know. Is he important?"

Wang shook his head. "Not really. Just someone I met when I came to see you."

Eddie frowned. He's always loitering around the place. I don't know how he gets away with it." He glanced down at his watch and began to shuffle in his seat.

"You need to get back?" Wang asked.

Eddie grinned. "My boss is very hot on time. Unlike some people's."

"Well, I appreciate your coming here. And if you have any further information . . ."

"Of course, Inspector. I do hope you can sort this out."

"I'll try my best."

Wang watched Eddie disappear into the alley, a river of black bikes and white-shirted pedestrians, then finished his tea in pleased, thoughtful silence.

"You've had Ren Hui's house under watch for two days, correct?" said Wang.

"Correct," said the young lieutenant from surveillance.

"And you've no reports of any activity?"

"Only lights going on and off, which we're convinced is an electrical timer. We've had barrel microphones on the place; I'll stake my life on it that the house is empty."

Wang nodded. "Is anyone else watching it? Apart from us, I mean."

"No evidence. We can't be sure, of course. Short of sending in a stalking-horse, we can't know."

"No. That's always the risk . . . But your men haven't seen anyone suspicious loitering around?"

"No, sir."

Wang paused for thought. "Right," he said suddenly. "We go in tonight. Tell your men to watch out for us. If they see anyone else taking an interest, they are to fire a pistol—two shots—abandon cover and move in. Understood?"

"Yes, sir," the lieutenant replied. There was hesitancy in his voice.

"You disapprove?"

"No, sir. It's just . . . Regulations . . ."

"Bloody Internal Security! They don't want anyone carrying weapons, right?"

"Yes, sir."

"Just because they want to be the only people in civilian clothes carrying guns . . . I don't see why you had to mention this operation to them at all."

The lieutenant looked embarrassed. "I was asked, sir. They like to know who's spying on whom."

"Interfering busybodies. This is a CID operation. You take your orders from me, not from some deskbound ideologist round the corner on Zhengyi Lu. Understand?"

The young man smiled.

"A pistol shot's still the best warning signal around," Wang went on. "Take a gun. I shall."

Nobody looked twice at the two men in baggy Mao suits and scuffed trainers entering the dingy *hutongs* of Chongwen. The taller, younger man had a patched canvas bag slung over his shoulder which clanked as he moved. The other was chain-smoking Panda cigarettes. A few minutes later, the area's power cut out—a common enough occurrence; the capital is bedevilled by power shortages. The smoker looked at his watch and nodded with satisfaction.

At the end of Pickaxe Alley, the men stopped to talk to a cyclist carrying out an emergency puncture repair.

"Seen anyone?" Wang asked him.

"Not a soul."

When they got to the door with the stone lions, they stopped again. Silence fell. Then footsteps. A man emerged from the shadows and asked Wang for a light.

"You've double-checked the back?" Wang asked him.

"Yes, sir. No ground-floor entrances: you'll have to go in through the front. Second window from the right is a kitchen. That looks the easiest access."

"And how about the other inhabitants of the yard?"

"All asleep."

"Good. And you've got your gun?"

The man grinned.

"Let's move," said Wang.

Lu walked across to the front gate and made a cup with his hands; Wang placed his foot in it and heaved himself up.

"Bugger! Glass." The inspector pulled off his cord-lined jacket and laid it across the jagged pieces of old bottle set into the top of the wall. On a signal, Lu pushed extra hard; in a moment Wang was over the obstacle and had dropped down into the corridor below. Lu, aided by the lieutenant, came lumbering after—a muscular fellow but not supple, Wang thought.

All that Western weightlifting; no *taijiquan*, no *qigong* . . . The
young man thudded on to the concrete.

"Sorry, sir!"

Wang glanced edgily round. Nothing stirred. They made
their way into the courtyard proper.

The black outline of Ren Hui's house stood out against the
pinkish glow of the city sky. Wang let his eyes accustom
themselves a little more to the darkness, identified the kitchen
window then dug into the bag, feeling for the necessary tools.

"OK," he whispered. They tiptoed across the yard. Wang
took out a can of sweet-smelling gum and smeared it over the
windowpane. He pressed a folded jute cloth on to it. They
waited a long, breathless minute while the gum hardened.

"Hand me the cutter."

Smothering the noise with another cloth, Wang began working round the window frame. The little battery-driven motor
sounded like a chainsaw, though he knew it was inaudible
more than ten paces away. When the job was done, Wang
pulled gently at the cloth-fold. There was a crackle of putty
and the pane slumped into his hands. He shone his torch
through the hole.

"Damn!" Between the window and the kitchen floor was
a sink full of crockery. It took Wang several minutes to re-
move the most precarious items, pull himself through the window, cross the flimsy modern sink unit and get his feet on to
solid floor. Then he paused, took three deep breaths and
checked his watch.

No panic. Still forty-five minutes till the lights came back.

Lu began to climb in.

"Careful!" A teacup began rolling towards the edge. Wang
reached forward and caught it as it fell.

"Sorry, sir."

They were both inside the house.

"We'll try downstairs first," Wang whispered. They padded
out into the hall—the bolts on the front door, Wang noticed,
had been fastened from the inside—then into the room where
Ren had received them. Wang ran his torch round the walls.

"*Ai-ya!*"

The room had been stripped of everything valuable.

Carpets, jade, tapestries: everything that Wang had noted as being of worth had gone. Even the drinks cabinet . . . The inspector gazed around in astonishment for at least a minute, then took control of himself and set to work on the few remaining items of furniture. A filing drawer rolled open; it was empty. A drab, modern desk had been searched but left full of bills, correspondence and cuttings about Jasmine's musical career—Wang bundled a selection into his bag, then shook his head.

"Let's try through there."

A utility room contained various electrical goods and a shelf full of drink. Beyond it was a small, simply furnished music room. Another quick search: nothing of interest.

"Let's try upstairs."

Halfway there, a stair creaked. Both men froze. No sound followed. They resumed their climb, emerging on a landing with three doors. Wang told Lu to stay and keep lookout, and tried the left-hand one. Jasmine's bedroom. A Western pop group of indeterminate sex posed above her desk; European and African models in huge hats and minute skirts grinned and pouted round the walls. Jackie Chan stood guard at the door. The Chinese star hadn't done a very good job—this room had been subjected to a manic search. Papers lay everywhere, drawers had been pulled open and ransacked. A clasp file marked "personal" lay pathetically open in the centre of the room. Wang glanced through it. Poetry in English, possibly words to songs; some work, signed as her own, in Chinese.

> "The cranes are calling in the mountains,
>   The wind answers through the pine trees,
>   The deer runs free in the forest.
>   In the city, young men and women are
>   fasting for freedom."

It was dated 27th May 1989.

Wang nodded. Nice juxtaposition; three symbols of longevity, then youngsters risking their lives. Ren Yujiao might be the daughter of a Triad Enforcer, but underneath she was clearly a woman of sensitivity and intelligence. He wondered for a moment how deeply she had been involved in the Beijing Spring: had the mess in this room been caused by the *Ke Ge*

Bo? There had to be a reason . . . Wang turned his attention to the singer's desk. It was unlocked: inside were a clutter of cassette tapes, more poetry, letters and photographs. He began reading, then checked his watch.

Don't take too long.

An inner drawer was half-open; Wang pulled at it, and it wouldn't budge. He moved on—but his curiosity had been aroused. He tugged harder, until it popped out from its seating. A sheet of cardboard that had been wedged down one side flopped into view. On it was a montage, of a photograph and a newspaper cutting, the latter dated 4th January.

SPARKLING PERFORMANCE AT
PEOPLE'S THEATRE
From time to time, even the most respected pieces of repertoire need a fresh approach. Last Thursday, the troupe *Shengli* from Tianjin gave a dazzling new interpretation of Lady Zhaojun . . .

Then Wang let out a cry. The photograph, a Polaroid, showed Jasmine and a man holding hands. They were standing in Dazhalan Alley, about a hundred yards from the theatre. She was looking away from the camera—uncharacteristically shy, or unwilling to be captured on film? The man was Xun Yaochang.

"Found something?" Lu hissed.

"Yes."

"What?"

"A piece of evidence. But you're on sentry duty. You shouldn't be listening to me."

"Sorry, sir."

Wang put the card in his bag—then shook his head and transferred it to his jacket pocket. Then he sat down on the bed and thought. He returned to the file and ran through the poetry till he found a more recent verse.

"Bright lights sink into the bitter sea;
    The bird of love flaps its wounded wings
    How much strength has it left?"

28th February. This year.

Enough to kill? For revenge, in disguise—her eyes behind gangster shades, her hair hidden under a Mao cap? It was suddenly possible—probable, even. Or was that what somebody wanted him to think?

Yes, that was it. Surely. Someone had meant him to find this little memento. Who? Why? He shook his head, then looked down at his watch again. Time was running out. He worked his way methodically through the desk, then checked other hiding places—nothing interesting. He crossed to Ren's bedroom. Nothing there, either. The third door led into a bathroom. Medicine cabinets can be the most revealing places in a whole house. He opened it—

"Wang!" Lu's voice was high and edgy.

"What?"

"There are people in the courtyard. Coming this way."

"Oh. And you haven't heard the warning signal?"

"Of course not."

The inspector stood stock still and listened. There were several sets of steps, heading straight for the door. Then silence. Scraping. A whisper. A squeak of glass told Wang that they had found his way in. Crash! That teacup hadn't lasted the night after all.

Think fast.

Wang did so, then whispered: "They don't know where we are. We must wait for them. And attack only if they come upstairs. Hide over there. Take the third, not the second man. I'll deal with one and two."

The two policemen crept into hiding places either side of the top of the stairs. Downstairs, the men clomped around the kitchen, crossed into the hall and kicked down the door of Ren's reception room. Someone fired a pistol: Wang gave his revolver a reassuring tap, while still hoping he wouldn't have to use it.

What do they want? What are they doing here?

The intruders stopped moving around and began whispering to each other. Wang felt sweat begin to prickle under his arms, down his back, round his crotch. He tried to move a little, but dared not make any noise. He glanced at his watch: hell, only six minutes of darkness left.

Come on. Get out. Or come up here and fight.

Five minutes.

Four.

Suddenly the voices were loud again and a torch-beam stabbed up into the gloom of the landing. The men began to climb the stairs. Wang was too busy counting steps to feel afraid. Eight, nine, ten . . .

The inspector sprang out on to the landing with a blood-curdling yell. Inches in front of him, a man holding a Type 51 Tokarev automatic froze with terror. A chop to the neck had the fellow tumbling down the stairs, bowling over his colleague—who was also armed and began firing in a blind panic. The third intruder, still at the foot of the stairs, pointed his torch at the action: Wang saw the gun on the top stair, threw himself at it and grabbed it, rolling out of the line of fire as he did so. A bullet fizzed past his shoulder and crunched into the plasterwork behind him: he stuck his hand round the banisters and fired his own Type 77 into the stairwell.

"Get him! Get him!" the third man shouted. There was panic in his voice.

"You fucking get him," number two replied, and received a bullet past his head as a reply.

"They're on the run," Wang muttered. Time to counter attack? From downstairs came the sound of the door bolts being forced open. Yes—they were retreating. Wang was just about to charge forward, when he heard the sound of running feet in the courtyard outside, coming towards the house.

No, they were letting in reinforcements.

"Get back into Ren's bedroom," he hissed at Lu. He fired another random shot down the stairs to cover his colleague's retreat. A yelp of pain told him he'd been lucky: the torch flashed away to the wounded man, giving Wang time to escape, too.

Back in the bedroom, the policemen were safe. For the moment. Wang picked up a chair, carried it noiselessly across the thick carpet and jammed its back under the door handle.

"Try the window," he whispered. "But don't make a sound!"

Lu did so. "It's locked, sir."

"Try forcing it."

"They're up there!" Wang heard the third man tell the reinforcements.

"It won't budge, sir."

Wang paused for a second. To smash the window would give their position away. To cut the glass in silence would take far too long. To stay and fight against superior odds was to run a terrible risk, especially—

"Break the lock!"

Lu banged the frame with his fist, then shook it, then kicked it.

"It won't—"

"Shoot it!"

"They're in the right-hand room!" Wang heard a voice cry. A moment later, someone's weight thudded against the door. The chair held. Lu fired twice: there was the sound of crunching wood and shattering glass. The window swung open. But at the same moment, another force slammed into the door. Wang's torch picked out the legs of the little bedside chair snapping like matchsticks and the catch of the lock tearing away from the door jambs.

Nothing else for it: the inspector hurled himself at the door as it swung open: again, his timing was perfect, catching the intruder the moment he entered. The two men crashed to the floor. A second man dived into the mêlée—and Lu was upon him at once. Wang was banging his opponent's head against the floor. Lu had his adversary reeling under a rain of punches. Someone began shouting: "We're outnumbered!" The intruders were in a total panic yet again; Wang's gamble had succeeded.

The lights went on.

Noiseless, instant and catastrophic, that changed everything and both sides knew it. The leader of the original raiding party entered the room with a swagger.

"Anyone moves, and I shoot," he said. "Tiger, get these bastards and tie them up. They've got some explaining to do."

"So have you," Wang thought. But there was no arguing with the gun pointing straight at his chest.

"Stand up," the boss said. Wang obeyed, his movements slow and deliberate, like *tai-chi*, to calm himself. What had happened to Lieutenant Huai and his colleague? Even if the

raiders had slipped past them, they should have heard the
shots. They should be here any moment. But there was no
sign of them. They had been immobilized: Wang and Lu were
fighting alone.

A trick—that was the only way out.

The man that Wang had slugged was on his feet now, and
rubbing his head. "Did I hurt you?" Wang asked.

The man turned and glared. Wang smiled, then spat straight
in his face. The man's face filled with fury, and he slammed
a punch into Wang's stomach.

"That'll do," said the boss.

Wang slumped theatrically to the floor, and the man followed him down, still yelling.

"Let me get at him!"

"*I said that'll do.*" The boss glared at his man. "Stand up,
both of you."

The man obeyed. Wang didn't.

"I said both of you."

Still no movement.

"Get him up," said the boss. The man began pulling at the
inspector's jacket; Wang went limp, as limp as he could—
then grabbed his assailant's neck, pulling the fellow across
him and forming a shield between him and the gun. Lu
watched uncomprehending for a split second, then understood:
a perfect *wushu* kick sent the weapon flying across the room.

The boss dived for it. Lu was ahead of him and grabbed his
outstretched arm inches short. Then grabbed the gun: the boss
gave him a punch in the ribs that sent him rolling across the
floor, but the young policeman held on to the gun. The boss
looked up. He knew at once he had lost his advantage.

"Run!" He leapt to his feet.

Wang's assailant paused to kick him in the ribs, then turned
and followed his leader. Lu sat up and fired: the bullet vanished into the door jamb. Wang tried to stand but flopped
forwards on to his face. The pain in his ribs was unbearable—
great waves of it, flowing up into him like electricity.

"Get them!" he moaned: Lu was up and out of the room
in a moment. Wang lay on the ground, gnashing his teeth;
dimly he heard a gun go off—he hoped it was Lu's—then the
sound of a door slamming shut. Then silence.

• • •

"Are you all right, sir?"

"Yes," said Wang, though his chest felt like someone had stabbed him. "Help me to my feet."

Lu did so.

"Did they all get away?"

"I'm afraid so, sir."

"Bastards."

The two men made their way painfully downstairs, and out into the yard, Lu clutching the bag of evidence like a child with a favourite toy. They were halfway across the yard when a figure emerged from the shadows. It had an automatic pistol trained on them.

"Put that bag down."

Wang heard the click of a safety catch. He tried to think of a way out—create a diversion!—but his brain was exhausted with pain.

"Do as he says, Lu," he said.

"Sir, I—"

"He means business."

The constable did as he was told.

"Now over against the wall," said the man.

Surely he wasn't going to risk two homicides; he had the evidence, after all.

"Tiger, leave us. I don't want witnesses."

Think. Think.

"And you, little boy. Run away. Come back with anyone, and your boss is *definitely* dead."

Lu looked at Wang, who nodded. "Do as he says." Lu didn't move. "That's an order."

Lu crept slowly out of the courtyard. The two men were alone. For a moment, Wang had this fantasy, that the Tokarev pointing straight at his heart would lower, that his assailant would grin, produce a police badge and let him into some huge secret.

None of these things happened.

"My boss doesn't like people who enter his house without permission—" the man began. Then light flooded into the quad. A door was open, and an old woman was shouting.

"What's going on here? Who are you?" She spotted the gun. "Help! Police!"

More lights came on. The man spun round, took aim at the lady—then cursed. He grabbed the bag and fled off into the darkness, while the lady began advancing towards the inspector. She had a large meat cleaver in one hand.

"We've had enough from people like you round here! I'm calling the police."

"I am the police!" said Wang. Then the yard began spinning round and round, and the ground rose up. It wasn't hard, it was welcoming and warm, the embrace of oblivion . . .

7

Wang lay still and watched as a nurse in a round, white cap hurried past, her heels clicking on the stone floor. Down the far end of Ward Five, International Peace Hospital, a private who had had his leg blown off in a training exercise was having another of his fits.

"It's still there! I know it's still there!"

The occupant of the bed next to Wang's, a colonel in Political Education here for a gall bladder operation, tutted. "Noisy bastard," he muttered, then went back to his comic book.

Wang let his gaze return to the cracks on the ceiling. But he knew them all. The one that looked like a map of China, but not quite, was beginning to irritate him.

"I'm better!" he told himself, and sat up, eager to take command of his life again. A stab of pain flashed across his chest.

Be patient.

When Wang was allowed visitors, the first one was his colleague Inspector Zhao.

"You *are* looking rough," said the new arrival. "Have some of this." He glanced around conspiratorially and handed Wang a bottle of Yantai brandy.

"My favourite!" Wang took a sip. "This is a marvellous present." Another sip. "Quite marvellous!" Then he heard footsteps, and slipped the bottle under his pillow. "What news from work?" he asked quickly.

"Everyone's been saying what a great job you've done. It's the talk of the department."

Wang looked puzzled.

"She's confessed. Didn't you know that?"

Wang sat up with a jolt, gave a cry of pain and sank back on to his pillows.

"That photograph you found—Jasmine and Xun Yaochang. It was obvious." Zhao grinned. "Wei put out a warrant for her arrest—but in fact, she walked in to a station in Dongcheng yesterday and handed herself over."

Wang pulled out the bottle and took a swig. "Handed herself in? Yesterday? In Dongcheng?"

Zhao shrugged. "My guess is that Ren's men came back after you'd gone, and turned the place upside down. When they realized you'd got the evidence, she did the sensible thing. You know how much more lenient courts are with people who admit their own guilt. Even in murder cases."

Wang sank back on to his pillows. So she had been hiding out in Dongcheng. In a Triad safe house, no doubt. Any point in searching the area? None at all, if she was really confessing. He sighed. He'd been sure that evidence was planted. It seemed he'd been wrong. It wouldn't be the first time in his police career.

"How's Lu?" he asked, with resignation in his voice.

"Back on duty. Upset, of course. Secretary Wei gave him a dressing down for 'bourgeois sentimentalism.' "

"Typical. Wei ought to find someone his own size to pick on . . . Any hope of catching those bastards who jumped us?"

Zhao grinned, which meant, not much. "They left a gun, but it didn't have prints on. We're trying to trace it, but you know what it's like with those old Tokarevs. They've been sloshing around the underworld since the Cultural Revolution . . . We've looked for prints in the house: just Ren Hui and his daughter. And the only bullet we've found so far comes from a Type 77. Yours?"

Wang nodded.

"Naughty. Our political masters in Zhengyi Lu won't like that."

Wang winced. How he hated the fact that ISB Headquarters were in Justice Road.

Zhao smiled. "I'd have done exactly the same on a mission like that, too. So would any working policeman. And Chen needs you back on the Huashan case. He'll get a memorandum from IS; he'll make a little speech then forget all about it." Wang's colleague shook his head. "You're lucky. You're in favour at the moment. I got a roasting for my self-criticism."

"You did?"

"They let me rejoin in the end, of course."

Wang had forgotten about the new campaign: Strengthen the Party. He was a lot less confident than Zhao about his own chances of getting through unscathed. Would they let him back into the Party at all? Wang began searching for a new topic. Then one of the younger nurses, Miss Lin, appeared, smiled at Zhao and pointed to the ward clock.

"I'm sorry. We have to be strict with visiting hours. Come a bit earlier next time."

"I shall," said Zhao with a smile. He turned to Wang and winked. "D'you think they'd let me in here for a few days?"

Miss Lin laughed. "You have to do something brave and patriotic first."

The colonel with the gall bladder grunted and turned over another page of his comic book.

Next day, it was Lu's turn. The young man strode up to the bed and handed over a box of dried plums in liquorice and one of those trashy novels about Martial Arts masters. Then he grinned nervously. "We really showed those guys, didn't we, sir! Two against—how many was it? Four? Five?"

"Five," Wang replied. The memory of the violence lingered in his mind like an unpleasant taste.

"That's teamwork! Real men do the fighting: bureaucrats sit behind desks."

"True." Wang was about to quote Sun Tzu—"To subdue the enemy without fighting, that is the mark of a great general"—but thought better of it.

Silence fell.

"So you're getting better?" said Lu.

"Slowly."

"Good. It's not the same without you."

"That's nice to hear."

"Paperwork. No action." The young man paused. "How did you know where to look for that photograph?"

"I didn't," said Wang. "It was just luck."

Lu looked disappointed. "Well, she's confessed, anyway. Zhao must have told you . . ."

"Yes. Don't let it upset you."

"I'm not upset. She was a bad element."

"I thought you were going to re-educate her."

Lu blushed. "That's really a job for the state, isn't it?"

"The bird flaps its wings and is gone."

"Sorry?"

"It's a poem."

"Ah."

There was a pause.

"Don't take any notice of Secretary Wei," said Wang.

Lu looked puzzled. "He was right to criticize me. He's a senior Party official."

"He's a bully."

More puzzlement. "You do say strange things sometimes, sir. Next you'll be saying the Army shouldn't have gone into Tiananmen Square!"

Wang glanced at Lu's presents—he hated liquorice, almost as much as trashy novels—and felt a sudden rush of affection for the young recruit; together with a sadness at the changes Lu would have to undergo in order to fulfil his ambition and become a real man, "like cut bone, polished horn, carved jade, ground stone . . ."

"Teamwork!" he said with a grin.

Next day, Team-leader Chen came to visit, without a present.

"Well done!" he said in a loud voice. "Our team is the talk of the department. Secretary Wei made a personal visit to the office the other day to offer his congratulations."

"That was nice of him."

"We can't wait to have you with us again," Chen went on. "Your skills will be in particular demand."

"I'll be back at work as soon as I can."

"Good. It's urgent."

"It will take some time, though."

"Of course. But there is a lot of work to be done." The team-leader lowered his voice (the colonel next door leant over to listen and nearly fell out of bed). "You shouldn't have taken that gun on the mission. Given the circumstances, I shall overlook the matter. But rules are rules. When can you start?" he added in his loud, official voice again. "Next week?"

"No. Next month."

Chen looked horrified.

"I've broken two ribs."

Chen leant forward. "There have been two more thefts," he whispered.

"One break nearly punctured my lung."

"Things are getting, er, serious. We need all the manpower we can get!"

"Haven't the constables been doing the filing properly?"

"They've been doing fine. I'd, er, like you to come and join the team at Huashan. On-site investigation."

Wang's expression lightened. At least some good had come out of the Xun affair. He wondered how far he could push his newfound favour. "I want to do some investigating of my own."

"Policing's a team business. What had you in mind?"

"To take a little time to look around the site; to talk to the people who work there . . ."

"Everybody's been interviewed. Several times."

"I know. I've read the transcripts. But this would help me settle in. That way, I'll be able to get back to work quicker."

Team-leader Chen looked at him suspiciously. Then sighed. "What sort of time did you have in mind? Next week?"

"I'll do my best," Wang replied.

"Do," said Chen. There was a look of desperation in the team-leader's eyes. Two more thefts in a week . . .

"No visitors today?" said Miss Lin.

"No."

"Haven't you got a family?"

"Yes, but—" He paused, thought of telling the truth, then

made up a story. It was partially true: his wife *did* now work in Shanghai, his son was at school there. He didn't add that Mei now lived with an official in the Ministry of Finance.

"They should come to see you," the young nurse said. "I think it's awful." Then she reddened. "Have I said something I shouldn't?"

"Not at all," Wang replied. He found himself smiling with pleasure at her reaction. She cared. Now she was smiling too—a full, simple smile, the sort of smile you got back in Shandong province.

Wang hadn't felt himself moved by a woman for ages. The pain of all that business with Mei had put up a barrier, one he hadn't even admitted existed.

"It's lust," he muttered to himself once she was gone. "Don't fool yourself it's anything else!" Anyway, she probably had a boyfriend half his age. He should find himself a nice widow, a daughter of a Long March veteran, with good contacts. Someone who loved Beijing Opera, folk song, classic novels and proper Chinese food.

Wang reported for duty at HQ exactly a week later. He sat on his hard wooden chair, staring round at his office. The maps; the cabinets; the striplight, now emitting a low, persistent buzz. And, of course, his calligraphy-scroll. *Zheng yi*, justice. He thought of the Xun Yaochang case.

Forget it. It's solved. You've done well . . .

But *is* it solved? Did Jasmine really kill Xun?

When Team-leader Chen appeared from a political sub-committee meeting, Wang told him that he wanted to see Ren Yujiao again. Chen's usual post-Party-business grin collapsed at once.

"You can't be serious. Why the hell do you—?"

"There are one or two details that I have to clear up. It's important."

"So is our work at Huashan. Anyway, this isn't a Public Security case any longer. It's all in the hands of the People's Prosecutor."

That evening, Wang put a call through to the People's Prosecutor.

•   •   •

Jasmine Ren sat huddled in a corner of the cell, on a hard wooden seat next to a half-eaten bowl of rice. Gone was her *qipao* and make-up—the performance was over; the reality, of a spoiled child who had smashed what she couldn't have, had reasserted itself.

"I'd watch out, sir," said the warder, closing the grille. "She's a wild one."

"Thank you," Wang replied coolly. "I know how to look after myself."

The door swung open and the inspector walked in. His nose wrinkled at the smell of sweat and damp.

The prisoner barely glanced at him. "What d'you want?" she mumbled.

"Just to ask a few questions . . . My name is Wang. Wang Anzhuang."

"I've said everything, haven't I?"

"Have you? Everything?"

"Everything."

Wang paused. "So you really killed Xun Yaochang?"

" 'Course I fucking did. It was what he deserved. Cheating little shit . . ." She looked up for the first time in the interview—Mei's eyes—and her expression changed at once. "I've seen you before, haven't I? Where was it . . . ? Oh, yes. You came to do business with my father just before all this happened. Don't tell me you're a sodding dog—"

Next moment the rice bowl was hurtling past Wang's ear, and Jasmine was on her feet and screaming at him.

"You cheating bastard! You made all this happen!"

She lunged at him: Wang half-dodged out of her way, but her nails tore into his sleeve. A second wild-clawed sortie was aimed at his face: Wang grabbed her wrists, and thought he had her under control. The toe of a prison boot slammed into his shin.

"Animal!" Jasmine screamed. She kicked again. Wang's balance was going—

The door flew open and two warders rushed in, grabbing the prisoner and dragging her away to her corner. Wang tried to steady himself, but he was shaking.

"If you come here again, I'll kill you. I've killed once; I'll do it again."

She began to sob, and the warders backed away.

"I did warn you, sir," said one.

"Yes, you did." Wang shook his head sadly. "I guess I'd better leave her to you."

When he got up to his office, he began clearing his desk of all the documents relating to the Xun Yaochang case.

"Investigate Chao, scar-faced man at Qianlong," read a note. Yes, he'd wanted to check out that hotel. Something odd had been going on there, even if it was nothing to do with Xun. But that would have to be someone else's problem now. He scrumpled the note up and threw it into the bin.

8

The Volkswagen Santana Shanghai came bumping out of the spruce trees, crunched along the dirt road of the upper valley and stopped outside the barbed wire enclosure. Sergeant Fang, at the wheel, tooted the horn. The noise echoed along the massive grey rockfaces all round them. Nobody appeared.

"Hoot again," Chen said from the back.

The sergeant did so. More echoes. Then a gatekeeper ambled into view with a mug of tea in his hand. Chen wound down the window and shouted at him. The man mumbled something uncomplimentary under his breath, but let them in.

"They should pay us more respect," said the team-leader.

"Possibly," Zhao muttered, though he couldn't see why. What had they achieved?

Wang, who was sitting in the front next to the driver, stared up at the landscape ahead of him. A huge triangle of grey granite rose up at the head of the valley: Mount Huashan. Across its great south face was a diagonal slash of sandstone, as if the mountain had been in a fight with a furious, knife-wielding god. This slash was the site of the caves. Eleven hundred years ago, a group of monks had fled here to escape the persecution of the Emperor. Wang tried to imagine their feelings. They must have heard rumours about the caves to have come here, but how they must have rejoiced to see those rumours confirmed, to see that soft, red scar and to know that it would provide shelter for them. And for their treasures.

The Shanghai bumped down the rutted passage between the compound's neat rows of tin-roofed huts, pulling up outside one with a sign on the door: THE PEOPLE'S POLICE SERVE THE PEOPLE!

"Ten minutes to relax, then we prepare ourselves for another round of interviews," said Chen, stepping stiffly out of the car on to the hot, rocky earth.

"Waste of time, those interviews," Zhao muttered once Chen was gone. Wang was inclined to agree—but fortunately that wasn't his problem, for the moment, anyway. He got out, stretched—that rib hardly hurt at all—and took in a deep breath of mountain air. Was Beijing really so polluted?

"Cigarette?" said Zhao.

This, Wang told himself, was his chance to give up. Remember that Party document "Smoking and Health"? In these surroundings, he could fill his body and spirit with fresh, clean, natural mountain air.

"Yes, please," he said.

The two inspectors lit up, and stood looking round the walls of the valley.

"It's a beautiful place," said Wang.

"I suppose so. You stop noticing after a while."

"What's the view like from up there?"

Zhao shrugged. "Hills, valleys, mountains. All rather grey—there's usually a haze."

"Classic Chinese landscape!"

"Well, there aren't any willow trees or Taoist monks moping about, but I guess in a way you're right. Not my style, I'm afraid." Zhao shook his head. "Give me a nice modern scene—motor cars, decent houses, electricity."

The two men smoked a little longer.

"So you really have no leads at all?" Wang asked.

"No. We've got filing cabinets full of work rotas, inventories, timesheets, roll-calls, day-and night-books . . . Nothing seems to add up. We've had the phones here tapped; we've followed siteworkers on leave; we have spot-checks of people and vehicles in the vicinity."

"And none of the missing items has ever been seen again?"

"No. Well, except for that Buddha that went on sale in New York. What was the asking price? Twenty thousand US dollars? Thirty?" Zhao shook his head. "That's hundreds of thousands of yuan, for a bit of bloody stone."

Wang nodded. "Don't you have *any* suspects?"

"No. That's the problem. It could be anyone. You've read all their files; your guess is as good as mine."

"But when you see them as individuals—don't some of them look and act suspicious?"

"Chen says they all do—but that's just the way he interviews people. Me? I don't know. I prefer to seek truth from facts rather than to chase after hunches."

"And when the facts say nothing?"

"I wait until they do." Zhao chucked the rest of his Panda away. "I'm going in."

The old shepherd's path snaked up the eastern side of the mountain, bend after bend after bend. It ended where the sandstone fault—and the caves—began. A soldier guarded this point, a matchstick man perched what looked like a mile above the camp. Wang gazed up at this climb, took a series of deep breaths and reminded himself of the old Taoist maxim that a journey of ten thousand miles begins with a single step. Then he took that step.

The path made no concession to comfort; up, up all the way, sometimes sloping, sometimes hewn into rough steps, never free of rubble despite the efforts of two specialist pioneers whose job it was to keep it clear and safe. Wang's chest began to ache about halfway up, and he sat down for a rest. The view was already spectacular: the compound below had become a child's toy; peaks were beginning to emerge over the huge rockfaces that had surrounded Wang on arrival. Pine trees marked the narrow mouth of the valley, through which a winding dirt-track was the only exit to the outside world. No wonder this place had guarded its secret so well for so long—until now.

"ID?" said the guard, when Wang reached the top of the path. The inspector fumbled in his pocket and produced it.

"That's fine, sir. Carry on."

"Thanks." Wang grinned. "Mind if I rest here for a few minutes? That's quite a climb."

The guard looked at Wang with a superior expression. "Three hundred and twenty-four metres. The best I've done it in is twenty-eight minutes."

Wang looked at the fellow as if he were mad, then remembered the importance he had attached to fitness until—well, a couple of years ago. "That's very good," he said, and entered the guardpost.

Huashan Cave One had been of no archaeological interest, so had been commandeered by Security. It now had bunk beds, a short wave radio, a gas stove and a supply of water in a plastic barrel. A calendar featuring Shanghai movie starlets added a touch of homeliness: underneath it, a shaven-headed teenage recruit sat filling in a notebook in slow, carefully-formed characters. Next to him was a Type 56 Kalashnikov copy, complete with bayonet.

"That's the day-log you're doing, is it?" Wang said to him. "Mind if I have a look? I've been off the case for a while."

"We're not supposed to show them to anyone."

"Not even police inspectors?"

"I don't know." The young man shrugged. "I just do what I'm told."

"Give it to me. That's an order."

Each watch kept logs, which were collected and compared at regular intervals. Wang had read dozens back in Beijing; this was the first he'd seen on-site. It was no different to the others. A mystery noise on the upper path, that had turned out to be a rockfall. A sensor in Cave Fifty-four triggered off by bats. A porter on the path attacked by an eagle . . . Near the end was an entry in red.

Theft, reported 09.35 hrs. Site, Cave Sixty-seven. Object, stoneware figure of the goddess Guanyin, height 212 mm. Wang shook his head sadly: he'd seen pictures of this piece, one of the finest finds on the site.

"You search everyone coming off the mountain, don't you?"

"Oh, yes, sir."

"How thoroughly?"

"Very."

Wang didn't doubt it. And anyway, the searches wouldn't need to be very thorough to reveal items as large as Guanyin. He waited till he had got his breath back, then went out again and continued his ascent.

The path ran all the way along the fault-line, right across Huashan's south face. As on the first part of its journey, it was remorselessly upward-sloping. And as the south face was sheer, Wang had nothing to his left but a giddy drop into the valley. No wonder notices every fifty metres or so reminded people to PAY ATTENTION TO SAFETY! To his right were the caves. He'd seen pictures of the main ones, and recognized their gaping, hungry mouths. Cave Five, site of some wall carvings, one of which had been carefully removed by Professor Qiao and her team—then stolen. Cave Twenty-two, famous for its frescoes: Wang would go and look another day, when he had more time. In a gesture worthy of Chairman Mao himself, the cave next to it had been turned into a latrine.

Cave Forty-four was the largest. The monks hadn't used it—possibly they'd counted the caves, too; the Chinese words for four and death sound worryingly similar . . . Professor Qiao's modern, superstition-defying team had made it their headquarters. The site hoist operated from outside it; inside Cave Forty-four all finds—ones that hadn't been stolen, anyway—were carefully wrapped and prepared for their journey to the valley floor. Right now, there was nobody about except for a small, round man in a sun hat, busy polishing the already spotless housing of the hoist motor. Wang found this individual needed no prompting to talk:

"Everything important comes up or goes down here. Food, water, tools, empties, artefacts . . ." The man gave the housing a fatherly tap. "Sit down. Another half hour, and you'll see it work."

Wang couldn't think of many duller things than watching a hoist pull a box up on to a mountainside, but accepted the invitation. The thefts took place on the mountain, not from the camp. So how did the thief or thieves get their contraband off Huashan? If the checks at Cave One were as thorough as the young guard claimed, the answer was not via the path. This hoist was the next most obvious means.

". . . Of course I've made a bit of a speciality of this kind of mechanism," the hoist operator was saying. "Before this job, I was working on a site in Beijing. There were considerable technical problems, all of which I managed to overcome, of course . . ."

Wang soon realized the fellow was an egotistical bore, but had been a policeman long enough to know the value of casual conversations—or in this case, monologues.

". . . Just as I'd told them, of course, right at the beginning. And of course, guess who had to sort it all out . . ."

Wang tried to keep his attention on the operator's words, but at last the effort became too much. He found himself wondering what other means of transportation were available to the robbers. Some hidden route through the caves? Hardly likely. The path? It ran on up the fault-line, right to the mountain's south-west ridge, apparently. Did it continue round the other side? Supposing—

A buzzer was sounding.

"That means ready!" said the operator. "Watch this!" He pressed a button on the motor, and the two hawsers that had been curving gently down into the abyss began to straighten.

"What kind of weight will this be?" Wang asked.

"Average is two hundred kilogrammes. More sometimes. You'll be amazed how much stuff has to come up."

"And go down?"

"Of course."

The box left the ground. If it was as heavy as the operator said, the additional weight of something like the statue would not be noticed. If, of course, it could be concealed.

The box remained tiny for most of its journey, then was suddenly life-size and a metre or so away. Two students came out and grabbed it. Wang followed them into the cave and watched it being unloaded. Nothing of interest emerged, just diesel for the site generator, drinking water and bottles of chemical for the latrines. Even so, the whole process was carefully overseen by two security men. Once the job was complete, Wang spoke to them.

"You always watch the unloading this carefully?"

"Oh, yes."

"And the loading?"

"Of course."

"How much d'you know about Tang dynasty Buddhist art?"

The men grinned. Maybe they'd been asked this question before. "If there's anything old, one of the experts does the inventory."

"Any expert in particular?"

"Not really. Dr. Jian is up here most often, so it's usually him."

"Ah . . ." Jian was the second most senior academic on the site. His file was full of complaints—breaches of regulations, lack of cooperation, criticism of superiors—yet no disciplinary action had been taken against him.

Wang ran slowly through the system of inventories with the guard: loads were listed in triplicate; a copy was kept here, two sent down with the box. Down there, they'd be double-checked; later they'd all be married up and compared. The system appeared foolproof.

"Can you recall a time when the loading wasn't observed?" he asked. "A time when someone senior told you to get out?"

"No, sir."

"You're sure?"

"Oh, yes."

Wang walked over to the hoist box and checked it for a false bottom or sides. Silly idea. "How many of these boxes are there?"

"Don't know. Only one, I think."

"Naturally . . ." He watched as an archaeologist began re-filling the box with shards of pottery, describing each one in detail before wrapping it up in a page from *Enlightenment Daily*. When the box was full, the man summoned the students to carry it out; the hoist motor began running again and the box sank from view.

"I never told you about when I was working on the Asian Games Village," said the operator.

"You must do," Wang replied. "Another time."

About halfway along the sandstone fault was a small outcrop of rock. The caves beyond this were too small to be of archaeological interest, and the site's chief security officer, a

man named Wu, had declared this upper section of the path
out of bounds. A clutch of red characters daubed on the rock
like a political slogan reminded people of the fact. There was
nobody guarding the outcrop, however, and no physical barrier. Wang walked straight by on to the forbidden upper section.

The path narrowed almost at once. Wang glanced down at
the valley floor, and reflected that Wu had been quite right to
prevent people from coming up here. But the inspector had
done mountain training in the Army. Heights held no terrors
for him—as long as he was on solid earth, anyway; aeroplanes
were a different matter. He pressed on, and the path soon
widened out again.

There were still caves to his right. All tiny: too small for
the monks to have used, but still big enough to crawl into. On
impulse, Wang got down on his hands and knees beside one
and did just that. The interior was tinder-dry: no wonder objects lasted so well up here. He flashed his pocket torch around
him. Fissures of rock headed off in all directions. The thought
of a secret passageway down off the mountain came back to
him, though exploration revealed that this cave would not be
the start of one.

Wang crawled back out into the daylight with great relief,
dusted down his uniform and began to climb the path again.
He soon reached the top of the fault, where the sandstone
intersected the mountain's south-west ridge. The path ended
here: all around him, rock fell away into that mist-grey valley.
The only way on was up the ridge, to the summit. It didn't
look too hard or long a climb—though the price of a mistake
would be high.

Wang had the skills, but was he fit enough? He sat down,
and gazed at the sawtooth mountains that rose up all around
him like a frozen sea. There, to the north, was the Great Wall,
switchbacking its way across the horizon. In such a magnifi-
cent setting, a man can only excel himself: Wang set off for
the summit.

In less than ten minutes, he was at a point where the ridge
forked and levelled off to form a long, flat gully between two
spines of rock a few metres high. He had reached the top of
Mount Huashan.

Wang sat down, lit a cigarette and enjoyed his achievement. The summit was, he noted, a perfect fortress, walled, gated and with only one possible access route. A quote from Sun Tzu came to him: "On mountainous ground I position myself on the sunlit heights and lie in wait for the enemy." Perhaps if he sat here long enough, the thief would walk up and hand himself over . . . He gazed down into the valley: Mount Huashan's great south face curved gently, and the huts where Chen and his team were slogging through paperwork were now out of view, as were the lower caves. Wang sent the first, half-smoked Panda wheeling out into space, and lit another almost at once; he felt he had earned the feeling of achievement and serenity that came over him.

> "The sky is blue,
>   The world rolls slowly round . . ."

"Hey!" The two men were on the upper path; one had fieldglasses trained on him, the other was shouting.

"What's the matter?" Wang called back.

"You're not supposed to be up there!"

"Oh . . ."

"Come down!"

The inspector made his way slowly down the ridge to where the men were waiting.

"You need permission to go beyond that outcrop," said the one with the fieldglasses, pointing back down the path.

"Oh. Who from?"

"Chief Security Officer Wu, or one of the team-leaders. Didn't you see the notice?"

"I've got a job to do," Wang snapped, then reflected that he would be better off staying calm. An ally is an extra set of eyes and ears. "I'll get clearance next time," he said calmly.

The guard nodded. "This path gets very narrow in places."

"I've noticed." They began to walk back down. Any tension between Wang and the men soon dissipated: time for some questions. "How often do you patrol up here?"

"Quite frequently."

"Because people quite frequently come up on to this section without permission?"

"That's right. It's usually the archaeologists. You can't tell those bastards anything."

"Any archaeologist in particular?"

"Dr. Jian is the worst. He's forever digging around in the caves up here. It would suit us all fine if he fell off—but it's our job to stop that happening."

"But you stop and reprimand him?"

"Of course. Two days later he's back here again. I'm afraid he has good contacts."

"Does Dr. Jian come up here alone?"

"Sometimes. Other times he brings a couple of the students with him."

"But you've never, well, caught him with anything illegal?"

"Illegal?"

"A missing artefact, anything like that?"

"Oh, no. Would that I had!"

They walked past a cave, and Wang peered into it. He was looking forward to meeting Dr. Jian.

9

Dinner at Huashan was supposed to be a communal affair. In practice, eaters sat in groups—police, security, archaeologists, porters and site maintenance workers. Wang collected his meal: a bowl of noodles, cabbage and bean-curd, a purple preserved egg and a steamed bun. He found a table where he could sit alone and watch.

Dr. Jian was surrounded by a gaggle of students. Two female ones sat either side of him, listening intently as he told them about a conference he had attended at Leyden University in Holland. Wang watched him for a while, then turned his attention elsewhere.

Jian's superior, Professor Qiao, sat alone, reading a book. Her face was lined—she was in her sixties, now—but her expression was one of strange contentment. It was an expression Wang had seen before, on the faces of people who had undergone great suffering at an earlier time in their lives; the kind of suffering that either broke people or toughened them totally. In the professor's case, Wang knew the story. At the height of the Cultural Revolution, a gang of Red Guards had smashed their way into her home and pushed her husband off their fourth-floor balcony. Professor Qiao had been marched through the streets in a dunce's cap, locked in solitary confinement for a year, then set to clean lavatories in the institute where she had been a senior lecturer. She had always been a loyal Party member; her husband's crime was to have criticized Mao ten years earlier, during the brief liberalization of the Chairman's Hundred Flowers campaign.

Among a table full of security men, Wang recognized their chief officer. Wu was ten years younger than Professor Qiao, and his records said that he had done a number of relatively easy security jobs before this one. Wang was shocked by how old the fellow looked. CSO Wu could hardly hold his chopsticks steady. Then Wang thought of the thefts. It was bad enough investigating these mysterious crimes, let alone being the man responsible for preventing them in the first place. Professor Qiao was a survivor of misfortune: maybe Wu wasn't.

Like the inspector and Professor Qiao, Team-leader Hei Shou ate alone. Hei was the Party's man here—nominally in charge of every aspect of the operation; in practice in charge of nothing. Once a week he would lead Political Study sessions. The rest of the time, he would be sitting in an office, filling in forms. He could hardly be the thief—but was in the perfect position to control others doing that job for him.

There were, of course, fifty other people in this room, slurping the unappetizing canteen food. Any one of them could be responsible—hell, even one of Wang's colleagues (though, on reflection, that was unlikely, as the thefts had started a while before Beijing CID were called in). Yet Wang had a feeling that someone senior had to be involved. Someone who could pull rank in a difficult situation.

"Of course, I might be totally wrong," he muttered. There were tables full of fit young men and women, who probably wanted more out of life than an academic's or a soldier's pay could provide. Stealing the artefacts looked very easy—maybe one of them had the intelligence to have worked out a plan that went beyond that, that got the objects down to the camp, on to Beijing, out into the West where they attracted such fabulous sums of money . . .

Wang turned his attention to his food. It was getting cold. As it probably would have been revolting hot anyway, did that matter? He tore a piece off his bun. Proper *mantou* steamed bread should be sticky; this was as dry as the summit of Mount Huashan.

The inspector reminded himself that he had asked to be transferred here, and began to eat.

Dr. Jian was cataloguing pieces of broken pottery in the long main workroom. He didn't want to be questioned in front of his subordinates, so he and Wang went for a brief walk to the perimeter fence instead. It was a bright morning, and already warm: when summer came, Huashan would be a harsh place to live and work.

The inspector tried to introduce a note of informality into the conversation. "I often find it easier to talk in the open air . . ."

"If that means our conversation will be shorter, that suits me," was the doctor's reply.

"I'll be as brief as I can. I understand you sometimes venture beyond the official limits of the dig—"

"Is that what you've dragged me out here to talk about? Regulations? I get enough of that from the chief security officer. I expected something a little more stimulating from Beijing CID."

Don't get drawn in. "I'm interested why you make these little expeditions."

"I'd have thought the reason was obvious."

"Tell me, anyway."

"I'm an archaeologist. My business is looking for artefacts."

"But the monks never lived up there."

"True. But they were fleeing persecution. It's very possible that they hid things there. Special, sacred things. If you knew anything about history—"

"Have you found any artefacts there, Dr. Jian?"

"You know I haven't. But that doesn't mean there aren't any. There are a lot of caves on the upper section."

"It must be very time consuming to search them all. Have you discussed this extra activity with your superior?"

"Professor Qiao and I have a good working relationship. She trusts me enough to let me follow my intuition."

"And your team-leader?"

"Comrade Hei Shou? He knows nothing about archaeology. What's the point in talking with him?"

"How about your students?"

"I talk to them a great deal. That is my job, or part of it, anyway. Look, I don't understand where all this is leading."

"I'm just trying to get facts sorted out. I also happen to find the subject of your work interesting, but that's irrelevant."

Jian turned to his questioner. "You do?"

"I read one of your papers. 'Is the political and moral decline of the late Tang dynasty reflected in the period's art?' A desk job in Beijing can get very boring, you know."

Jian's face went through a series of emotions. "An intellectual . . ." he muttered at the end.

"My father was a peasant, but had a respect for learning. I believe your own background is not dissimilar."

Jian nodded. "Is it a crime, in the modern world, to want to make something of your life?"

"That depends on how you do it," Wang replied, then realized he had gone too far and held up a hand. "That's not an accusation. You can pursue your ambition any way you like as far as I'm concerned. My only concern is with the thefts—to know the truth. I want your help in doing that."

They walked on in silence for a while, then the doctor began to talk. He was busy in the main caves most of the time, he explained, but occasionally sneaked past the outcrop on to the upper pathway. He was working his way slowly up towards the summit: so far he had searched the eight lowest out of bounds cave systems. He had in fact found a few scraps of pottery, but had not announced the fact as they were of no value.

"I sometimes wonder if the security personnel here want us to succeed," he said. "They seem to have found a perfect way of combining minimum effectiveness with maximum interference. Don't go here! Don't do that!"

"They have responsibilities," Wang put in.

"They enjoy interfering. They even spy on us. CSO Wu watches through a telescope. Someone is tapping the phone. And only the other day, I was working late on a report; there was a noise at the window—I turned round and someone was running off."

"The guards patrol the compound all night, don't they? It was probably just one of them, bored and a little curious."

Dr. Jian shivered, as if even the memory of the incident scared him. "Maybe. But I wish they'd catch this thief, not go round frightening people." He glanced down at his watch. "Look, Inspector—I'm sorry if I was rude earlier. You've probably seen how things are here. Everybody suspecting everybody else. It gets to one. Then your team-leader sits us down in his hut, and virtually accuses us of the crime . . ."

"He's only doing his job. But I accept the apology."

"Good." The doctor glanced at his watch again. "Can I go?"

"For the moment."

Jian didn't move. He stared at the ground, then looked Wang in the eye.

"There's one more thing. I've said this to Team-leader Chen, he didn't understand. You might. The objects being stolen—some of them are national treasures. That statue of Guan-yin, for example. Never mind how many millions of yuan it's worth in the West, it's worth more in China. It's ours. Our heritage, our soul. No Chinese archaeologist could steal it and sell it off to the highest bidder. If you knew the history of the subject in this country—the damage inflicted by foreigners at Dunhuang, the destruction we brought upon ourselves during the Cultural Revolution—you would know that. It's impossible."

Dr. Jian turned and walked off, leaving Wang to ponder if he should recommend him for this year's Golden Rooster award for best actor, or if the fellow had been sincere.

Chief Security Officer Wu's office was in a hut in a far corner of the camp, the corner from which was the best view of the mountain. Wang knocked on the door; a voice told him to come in; when he did so, he found the CSO peering through a telescope at the mountain-face. Wu turned towards his visitor.

"How can I help you?" Wu said, with such coldness in his voice that Wang was taken aback.

"I, er, just want a few words. About the section of the

pathway above that outcrop—the section you put out of bounds.''

"What about it?"

"I gather people still go up there."

"I can't stop them. I'd have to have men on guard there the whole time to do that. I don't have the resources. That's not my fault."

"No . . ." This was the wrong approach. Wang let his eyes rove round the hut—simple unadorned walls, the telescope, a rifle in one corner. "I also want to talk about the thief."

CSO Wu's eyes widened. "You know who it is? Congratulations. It's taken you long enough."

"I'm afraid not. But I was wondering if you had formed some view as to his, or her, identity."

"I might have done."

"Care to share your thoughts with me?"

"Not really."

"I gather my team-leader, Chen Runfa, hasn't made himself popular by his interrogation methods. Forthright, I believe he is—"

"Accusatory."

"But you must see that everybody has to be under suspicion. You're a security man; you must understand that."

"There's suspicion and suspicion. Chen interviews people as if it were 1972. 'You are guilty! Disprove it!' "

Wang nodded. "You're talking to me now, not him."

"You're all the same, you Beijing big shots."

Wang, who knew the CSO was a countryman, said: "I'm from Shandong, actually."

"You've lost your accent."

"Inevitable, over time."

"Not if you care about your home. Where are you from?"

"Nanping. Xintai county."

"Hill country. I'm a plains man myself."

Silence fell. This interview was not progressing well. Then CSO Wu seemed to relax.

"If you really want my opinion, it's one of those archaeologists. It has to be one of them, or one of my men, and *they* have security clearance. The archaeologists don't."

"There are others on the site with minimal vetting. What

about the porters? Or the man who operates the hoist?''

Wu shook his head. ''I also think our thief is clever. An intellectual. What did the late Chairman call them? 'The stinking lowest rank of humanity.' Your team-leader should spend less time harassing honest members of the working class and more time investigating those chicken-fuckers. That's my view.''

So the CSO had given the problem some thought after all: he wasn't as stupid as he tried to make out—even if he did equate intellectualism with homosexuality.

''And how do you think the thief gets the stolen goods off the mountain?'' Wang asked him.

''Smuggles them, I guess. My men don't always search the top people as rigorously as they should. You know how it is— Party members can cause trouble for an ordinary soldier trying to do his job.''

''But large items have disappeared.''

''Maybe those go at night. If I had enough men, I could mount a proper twenty-four-hour guard.''

''Nobody would descend that path at night, surely.''

Wu shrugged. ''Someone's getting the stuff off the mountain.''

Wang wasn't convinced that was necessarily right: maybe the thief was simply hiding them somewhere up there. At least one piece had been smuggled out, that was true; but all of them? However, he saw no point in sharing these thoughts with Wu. ''Who determines the size of your guard?'' he asked instead.

''I do. Within my budget. That's the problem.''

''And who determines the budget?''

''Hei Shou, the big Party man.''

Wang paused. Another glance round the office.

''Mind if I have a look through your telescope?'' he asked.

Wu didn't seem too keen on the idea, but said: ''No.'' He got up and began fiddling with the eyepiece. ''It's a good scope,'' he said finally. ''Look, there's Engineer Zhang polishing his bloody hoist motor again. You can even see the smug look on his face.''

Wang put his eye to the mechanism. Wu was right, about the telescope and about Engineer Zhang. He ran the scope along up the path, past the rock outcrop to the upper section, past those small caves, one of which Wang had crawled into—until the curve of the mountain's face took the fault out of view and there was nothing but bright blue sky.

"Useful . . . D'you have a radio link up to there, too?"

"Yes, but it's not reliable. I've complained about it enough times, but nothing gets done. Hei Shou again. I wonder what he does in that hut of his all day."

Wang nodded. Hei might be incompetent, or the problem might be insoluble. Some geographical locations seemed to play havoc with radio communication, as Wang had learnt in Vietnam.

"So this telescope is an important way of keeping watch on things?"

"When I'm not up on the mountain, yes."

"And have you ever spotted anything untoward?"

"Yes. Archaeologists, wandering up on to the most dangerous part of the pathway. No protection, no precautions. That bugger Jian's the worst."

Wang waited for Wu to say more, but he didn't.

"But you never see people loitering suspiciously around the theft-sites?" Wang said, after a pause.

"Sometimes. I send a man to check. It's always turned out to be harmless." Wu cleared his throat and spat into a bowl on his desk. "As I say—this thief is clever. Bloody clever. An intellectual, you see. He has to be. But he'll make a slip one day. Intellectuals always do."

"They fuck the wrong chicken," said Wang.

CSO Wu slapped his side and roared with laughter.

Before being given the job of archaeologists' team-leader, Hei Shou had been in charge of a factory. Quite a famous one: Shenchun Number Three Machine-Tool Factory had been one of the first enterprises in the People's Republic to be declared bankrupt. It hadn't been his fault: Hei's predecessor had run Number Three on strict Maoist lines. Quotas were always met; quality control was non-existent; nobody was ever dismissed except for political offences. So what if a day's output included faulty products? If the workers' consciousness was high enough, such trivialities did not matter. The notion of faultiness was a bourgeois one, anyway. A true Communist could make do with faulty equipment . . . Unfortunately, the factory's customers did not think this way: by the time Hei took over, the huge noisy concrete shed that was his empire was surrounded by piles of rusting, unwanted machinery. Then along came Deng Xiaoping's economic reforms.

Now he was here.

"Come in," said Hei as Wang knocked at the door of his office. Wang did so. The team-leader's desk was piled high with paperwork. "Sit down. How can I help?"

"I want to talk about money."

Hei looked surprised. "Money?"

"What sort of budget does this operation have? And is it keeping to it?"

The team-leader sat up and straightened the line of pens in his top pocket. "The People's Government attaches the highest importance to archaeological research, as part of the development of Socialist Spiritual Culture. However, in the current economic situation, financial controls must be exercised in all areas of activity—"

"It's in trouble?"

He looked at Wang suspiciously, then nodded his head.

"There was never enough funding in the first place. And thanks to these robberies, work is getting behind schedule. There are plans to close the whole operation down. We seal up all the caves and smash the path up the eastern flank. Maybe in twenty years, there'll be the resources to begin again."

"Who knows about this?"

"Me. Professor Qiao. And now you."

"Nobody else?"

Hei shook his head. "I wouldn't tell any other academics. It doesn't concern security at this stage. And none of your colleagues have asked." He paused. "Of course, anyone with any common sense can guess the rough situation. The thefts have meant more security; savings have to be made elsewhere. Work has had to slow down; the Ministry is getting concerned about the lack of progress. And everybody blames me."

Wang nodded sympathetically. "How much does it cost to run this operation?"

"Around fifty thousand yuan a week."

To Wang, that sounded a fortune. But so had the price that the stolen Guanyin had fetched in New York.

"Tell me about Dr. Jian," the inspector said after a pause. "Nobody seems to like him much."

"His colleagues do. He's an up-and-coming young academic. Very bright and all that. But he hates the likes of you and me. I guess it's all to do with—well, you know, Tiananmen Square and all that. He reckons anyone who's in the Party is directly responsible."

"He seems to be able to get away with making trouble."

"I know. He's got contacts in high places. People who admire his work. Apparently, he's a Marxist, and there aren't many of those left in academia. I thought we were all supposed to be Marxists—but I'm not as clever as Dr. Jian."

"I thought you knew those files backwards," said Inspector Zhao as he packed away for the evening.

"So did I," Wang replied.

"What are you checking?"

"Nothing."

The Chinese way of saying bullshit is "your words are like farts."

"OK, something. The phone monitoring."

"What about it?"

"Who knows which phones are bugged and which ones aren't?"

"In theory just us, Team-leader Hei Shou and CSO Wu. But you know how it is—you can tell, if you're on the look-out."

"The thief would be on the lookout."

"Ah—so you do have a theory."

Wang looked embarrassed. "Well, not a fully-fledged—"

Zhao was peering across his shoulder at the files. "Dr. Jian? Have you got something on him? That would be a perfect solution. Arrogant little shit."

Wang snapped the file shut. "My investigations are at a very early stage."

"Lucky you. Mine have been going on for months and got nowhere."

Wang's embarrassment returned. He knew how lucky he was, being able to follow his own leads and intuitions, not tied down by Chen's obsession with routine. Reading those reports, he sometimes found himself wondering if the team-leader wanted the thief caught at all . . .

"I'll buy you a beer at the canteen," he told his colleague. "Just give me another ten minutes."

Zhao's expression lightened. One of the compound huts had been turned into a mess room, where export-only *Tsingtao* beer was on sale. "Ten minutes," he said, and left.

The office door shut. Wang was alone with his thoughts. Motives. Greed, pure and simple? Or something more subtle? Supposing someone was stealing the artefacts, to sell them abroad—something the Chinese government would never do— to finance further work. Had Dr. Jian been trying to tell him that, in that little speech outside his workroom? Or was the doctor deceiving him, to conceal baser motives? The young archaeologist was clearly ambitious: maybe Professor Qiao stood in his way. A survivor like her wouldn't retire for many years yet. Unless she were forced out of tenure by a project that degenerated into a money-wasting farce . . .

Yet on the other hand, Dr. Jian's expeditions on to the upper mountain had a perfectly rational explanation. They were always carried on in full view of the camp. He seemed quite happy to cut a conspicuous, if unpopular, figure. So what if the fellow had the intelligence to notice the phones were sporadically tapped? You didn't have to be a thief to resent that.

There was also the business of the spying. Looking through the files, Wang had found several complaints by people who had been snooped on—some from young female students, who reckoned it was a pervert. If it was in fact the thief, why were they doing this, when all their work was carried on up the mountain? If it wasn't the thief, why spy on Dr. Jian?

Wang shook his head, glanced up at the clock—Zhao would be getting thirsty, and he didn't want to let his younger colleague down. He stood up, tidied his desk and put Dr. Jian's file back in Chen's green steel cabinet. The key turned easily in the lock—who else, he wondered, had keys apart from himself, Chen and Zhao? Did that matter? A lock as basic as this wouldn't take much picking by a professional.

Questions, questions; Wang had had enough for one day.

•   •   •

Music came floating out of the mess room, another of those sentimental Taiwanese ballads about lost teenage love. Wang walked towards its welcoming squares of yellow light. An idea floated into his mind—supposing Jian were carrying on with one (or more) of the students who seemed to admire him so much. That would explain why he was worth spying on. Would it explain why Dr. Jian wanted to tell the story? If Jian didn't know about the other incidents—maybe he'd been genuinely scared . . .

The drunkard staggering round the corner nearly bowled Wang over.

"Watch where you're going!"

The man glanced up; a look of terror filled his eyes; he turned tail and ran. On impulse, Wang gave chase; the man dodged and dived, then fell. Wang stood over him.

"Get up!" he ordered sternly. Then, when he saw who it was: "Are you all right?"

Chief Security Officer Wu got unsteadily to his feet. "You won't report me, will you? Not a fellow Shandong man. City folk don't know how to drink . . . Please."

"You can rely on me," Wang replied in dialect. The chief smiled, shook him by the hand, then stumbled off into the darkness.

10

Usually, after he had drunk a bit, Wang had the same dream. Of running from a phalanx of armed soldiers, but getting no further away from them. Last night, he and Zhao had put away several *Tsingtaos* and a few tumblers of *Maotai* spirit—but all Wang dreamt of was food: a bowl of decently-cooked rice, squidgy sea-cucumber stuffed with minced pork and ginger, deep-fried Yellow River carp in black rice-vinegar sauce . . . Then a siren started up, barging its way into the feast like an uninvited guest. It wouldn't stop; the meal became a memory; Wang sat up and rubbed his eyes.

Outside, figures were running. The scene was one of panic, like those air-raid practices in the 1960s when people had expected Soviet or American H-bombs any day. Wang threw on his uniform and staggered out into the early morning air.

"What's up?"

"Accident," said someone.

A crowd had gathered by the gate. He went over to join them.

"One of your guys," said another spectator. "Fell off the mountain . . ."

Wang, instantly cured of last night's excess, ran back to the investigation office. It was locked. His imagination raced. It wouldn't be Chen; the team-leader rarely left his office. If anyone went up the mountain, it was usually Zhao or Fang. Then Zhao appeared.

"What's it all about?"

"Don't know. Someone's fallen off."

Zhao raised his eyebrows. "Had to happen, didn't it? Those stupid bloody archaeologists . . ."

"It's one of ours, apparently."

"What?"

A party of men could be seen approaching the camp.

"We'll soon find out who," said Wang. The two policemen walked down to the gate, arriving at about the same time as the stretcher-bearers. The body was covered with a sheet.

"Where are you taking him?" asked Wang.

"Don't know, sir," one of the men replied. He looked pale and his breath smelt of vomit.

"Use the main workroom," said Zhao. "They'll have to stop fiddling with bits of pottery for the day."

A man ran ahead to warn Professor Qiao. Wang walked alongside the body.

"Who was it?" he asked the stretcher-bearers.

"CSO Wu, sir."

"Ai-ya!"

"Another of our generation," muttered Professor Qiao as the body passed by.

Inside, they cleared a space. Dr. Jian watched with interest.

"I think you should leave," Zhao told him.

"This is my workroom!"

Wang pulled back the cover. The fellow's face had been smashed beyond recognition. One of his thigh bones had jammed itself right up through his stomach.

Dr. Jian ran outside and was sick. Even Wang closed his eyes in automatic revulsion—then began to search the pockets.

Identity confirmed. Chief Security Officer Wu.

The man who had found Wu's body was a Private Ping. He couldn't have been more than eighteen; when Wang suggested he show him the place where he'd made the discovery, the lad looked less than enthusiastic.

"You'll have to get used to the sight of death if you're

going to be a soldier,'' Wang said as they walked across the dry upper valley.

"Yes, sir,'' Ping replied. He was lanky and delicate featured, not really the fighting type. Wang seemed to recall that Ping came from a good family: they had probably pressurized the young man into joining up.

Wang took him through his story again. "You'd gone for a walk, and heard a scream. You looked up, and saw Wu falling. Correct?''

Ping nodded.

"Did you look up, to see where he'd fallen from?''

"No, sir.''

As long as the lad didn't try and transfer from the Army to the police . . .

They reached the scree at the foot of the mountain. Ping pointed to a small, jutting rock caked with black blood.

"It was here, sir.''

"Yes.'' Wang glanced up at the mountain. "Is this where he actually hit the ground? A falling body can bounce or roll quite a long way.''

"Don't know, sir. I didn't see him land.''

The inspector began to clamber around the scree slope. He soon found a bloodstained dent in the pebbles. He thought of that jutting thigh bone again.

"Thank you, Ping: you can go. I'm sorry to bring you back here so soon.''

The young man scurried off. Wang worked his way methodically around the area, but found nothing. Then he turned and walked slowly back to his hut through the gathering heat.

Someone had put white tape on poles all round the spot from which the CSO had fallen. The afternoon brought a soft breeze puffing up from the valley; it made the tape flutter like bunting. Wang and a two-man patrol stood smoking Pandas and peering over the edge of the precipice.

"No one's tidied up here, then?'' he asked the patrol-leader.

"No, sir. Mr. Fen gave strict orders to leave everything untouched.'' Wu's deputy Fen had stepped smartly into his boss's shoes.

"Good. And they've been followed?''

"As far as I know, sir."

"Excellent."

The path had its usual thin cover of dust and pebbles: there hadn't been a fight. At the edge, a short section of newly-exposed rock showed what *had* happened: Wu had simply been standing too close to the edge, on a slightly overhanging lip that had given way. Why? The path was over a metre wide at this point; Wu should have kept to the inside. Instead, he'd broken a basic rule of safety, one that is drummed into mountaineers over and over again. Why?

The obvious answer. After-effects of last night's drinking. But why had he come up here at all?

"Who else was on the mountain early this morning?" he asked the patrol-leader, a sergeant.

"Just us, and the boys down in Cave One."

"You're sure?"

"As sure as I can be. I didn't see anyone else!"

"I didn't, either" the other patrolman put in.

"But you saw the chief?" Wang asked the sergeant.

"Yes. He just walked by."

"Did he look agitated?"

"No more than usual. He was always jumpy. These thefts got to him—I think he felt it was all his fault . . . And he had a chip on his shoulder about cities. He was a shit-shoveller; he was determined to show us city folk he was better than us."

An image sprang into Wang's mind, of the kind, hard-working people among whom he had grown up: peasants, shit-shovellers. Wang wanted to get a bucket of the stuff and shove the bastard's head in it. But he had a job to do. "So Wu put in a lot of extra hours, patrolling the upper section of the caves on his own?"

"That's right, sir."

"Which is what he was doing when he fell?"

"I guess so." The sergeant shrugged. "Who knows what he was up to. Shit-shovellers are all crazy, if you ask me."

An eagle flapped past. It was a welcome diversion. The junior patrolman in particular seemed fascinated by it.

"I've got this theory," he said suddenly.

The sergeant glared at him.

"What is it?" Wang asked, more to annoy his superior than out of genuine curiosity.

"I think he was attacked by an eagle, sir."

The sergeant moved to shut the lad up, but Wang stopped him. "No, let him speak. What makes you think that?"

"Well, Comrade Inspector. They get vicious if you go near them. Especially this time of year, when the chicks are in the nest. I've often thought, if one of them attacked you, and you were on that path, and you lost your balance . . ."

The sergeant glared at him.

"Interesting," Wang said.

"Eagles are intelligent birds, Comrade Inspector," the lad went on. "I read this piece in the *People's Daily* last year. Party cadres in mountainous Shuangfen county had trained eagles to deliver messages from village to village, thus saving valuable resources of fuel."

"Couldn't they use telephones?" said the sergeant.

"Don't know. Perhaps there weren't any. It didn't say in the article."

"They were probably too stupid to operate them." The sergeant launched into an impromptu comic turn—a man with a thick rural accent trying to figure out a telephone and failing.

"You have a bright young man here," Wang told him at the end. "Listen to what he has to say."

Cave Twenty-two was a good place to calm down. The Buddhist paradise, the City of Willows. Wang stared at the gold-haloed saints floating round a huge, smiling Buddha—and his thoughts went back to Beijing. The term was also used by the Triads, by people like Ren Hui and the dead blue lantern, Xun Yaochang. Xun who had been killed, everyone agreed, by Jasmine Ren, a rejected lover.

Wang had been trying to banish that case from his mind—and had done well in the last few days. But it wasn't going to go away that easily. He was thinking of Jasmine Ren, now, sitting in that cell. He was thinking of his interview with her—had he misunderstood her words; was there some coded message she had been trying to give him? Of course not. His intuitions had been wrong, that was all.

Anger, an emotion absent from the golden world in front

of him, suddenly filled his heart. He thought of the fight at Pickaxe Alley; of how little was being done to pursue the culprits. Where was Ren Hui now? Damn him to hell. And damn his daughter, for being so young and talented but giving in to the cheap lure of violence.

As he walked out of Cave Twenty-two, Wang met Inspector Zhao.

"Wang!"

"Zhao! What are you doing up here?"

"Same as you. Going to see where poor old Wu fell off the cliff."

"How did you know I was doing that?"

Zhao laughed. "I didn't—until now. D'you think he fell?"

"No idea. There's no evidence of a struggle or anything. It's a mystery." Wang gazed out across the valley. "Unless it's true—he really was attacked by an eagle."

"Eagle?"

"It's just a theory someone came up with." Wang shrugged. "The truth is, I haven't got a clue."

"As long as it's not murder," Zhao said. "That's the last thing we need here, now that—but you won't have heard, will you?"

"Heard what?"

"The news."

"What news?"

"Guess."

"Don't know."

"Try."

Zhao enjoyed little games like this. Wang was never any good at them. He knew he should say something witty, but always ended up sounding pathetically prosaic. Typical shit-shoveller. "I give up," he said.

"They've found one of the stolen pieces."

Wang gasped. "Where?"

"In Canton."

"Canton?"

"A tourist was trying to smuggle it over the border to Hong Kong."

"Hong Kong?"

"Chen's delighted. He wants to move the whole operation

down there, leaving just Fang here. Fang volunteered to stay—very noble.''

"Yes, I—''

"Seek truth from facts,'' said Zhao. "And at last, we have one!''

Chen was on the phone when Wang entered the office. The team-leader gestured to him to sit down, then resumed his conversation.

"No, I don't think that would be a good use of public funds. Simple accommodation will do us fine. A barracks? Perfect. An officer in the People's Police doesn't require luxury.''

"Zhao's told me the news,'' said Wang, when the call was over.

"Good, isn't it?''

"Yes . . .''

"I'm just finalizing arrangements. As the best linguist among us, Inspector Zhao will be going to Hong Kong. Wang, you and I will base ourselves at Canton. Sergeant Fang, Constables Lu, Tang and Han will remain at their current posts. We leave here at 05:30 hours tomorrow morning. Estimated time of arrival in Beijing is 08:00.'' Chen grinned. "I knew this would happen. Wait long enough, and criminals always make a mistake.''

The alarm, hidden under Wang's pillow, went off at half-past one. The inspector lay in silence for several minutes, listening for signs that it had woken anyone but him. Chen's snores from one partition gave a clear message; Zhao, on the other side, was a heavy sleeper anyway.

Wang got up and dressed. Tracksuit. Trainers. Gloves. And, in case of any trouble, shoulder-holster and Type 77.

The night was muggy, warm and still. Wang trod carefully: sound would carry easily.

Chief Security Officer Wu's office was a long way from the sleeping quarters, right out by the perimeter fence. Wang passed nobody on his way there. When he arrived, he sat motionless on the step and listened. The silence of Huashan valley was absolute.

The new security officer, Fen, had had a thick steel padlock fitted to the door. Wang didn't recognize the type—but he had plenty of time. He took a wire from his pocket and set to work . . . The moon went behind a cloud: Wang looked up. Still no one about. Back to the lock. Two more clicks . . . It sprung open. Wang grinned with pride at his handiwork: could anyone else on the site have done that?

Apart from a chair that had moved and a lingering smell of cheap sorghum wine, Wu's office was as Wang had remembered. The telescope by the window: Wu had fiddled around with it before letting Wang look through the lens. Why? The gun in the corner was a Dragunov sniper rifle: quite a weapon, possibly capable of picking someone off from the face of Mount Huashan. Wang shivered, then sat down at Wu's desk and began working methodically through its contents.

Papers on the top. Undisturbed. The handwriting was spidery and loose. The work of a worried man? It was also difficult to read in the gloom: Wang picked the papers up and put them in a lozenge-shaped pool of moonlight on the hut floor.

Memorandum, to Deputy SO Fen, re: rockfall, Section Fifty-eight.

Report from Patrol Three, re: failure of routine test of bleepers.

Security clearance for maintenance engineer to check hoist motor.

Sickness and overtime sheets for week ending Sunday 19th May . . .

Wang worked through the pile, then glanced at his watch. Half-past two. The perimeter guards usually set off about now: he slid the papers out of view and waited.

Two thirty-five.

Two-forty. Come on, boys . . . Then he heard the sound of boots. Someone cleared his throat and spat. A shadow fell across the window. For a moment, the inspector felt a tingle of fear—then the shadow was gone, and the footsteps receded.

Next, the desk drawers. They opened easily. The first contained inventories of finds, cave by cave—useful for the thief, but exactly what a security officer would need, too. The next contained rough paper and a notebook in which duty rosters had been worked out. Wu had divided his men into three categories: circle, square and triangle. Circles and triangles usually worked one of each in a team. One good man and one poor one? Good information for a thief, but good security practice too. Read on.

Chen Runfa, Team-leader. A triangle.

Wang Anzhuang, Inspector. A circle. And yesterday's date.

Wang began to note down any times when double circles and double triangles had been on duty together. He was soon analysing the data. Any patterns? Any correlations with dates and times of thefts? No, of course not. But why should there be? A theft could go several days without being detected. And if, as Wang suspected, Wu hid the items on the mountain, he could smuggle them off when he liked. How, he still wasn't sure, but that could wait . . . The circle-rated inspector didn't even notice his watch creep round to half-past three; he didn't even hear the footsteps of the approaching guards until they were right by the hut. Then the shadow was back, cutting across the window. Wang froze.

That book!

It was in the middle of the floor, where it gave off a soft white glow that could easily attract the attention of an alert man. And if a soldier *were* that alert, he would then wonder why he hadn't noticed the glow on a previous walk round, and at least flash a torch through the window. But if Wang moved to hide it . . .

The guards walked past. Wang gave them a while to be gone, then wiped the sweat off his forehead before getting back to work. He finished copying the significant combinations from the notebook. He cleared out the drawer—just a few scraps of paper with characters jotted on. *Take Corp. Hu off nights. Double guard, Cave Fifty-three*. Two seven-digit numbers: 5122831 and 6321275. The first one was the phone number of Public Security HQ in Beijing; the second . . . He'd find out. The third drawer was empty.

Five-to four. Chen and Zhao would be stirring soon: no sense in taking unnecessary risks. He put everything back as he had found it, took one last glance around, then tiptoed across to the door and left. The lock clicking shut sounded uncomfortably loud, but the noise echoed away into silence.

The moon hung low over the mountains as Wang made his

way back to his own quarters. The tin roofs of the huts glowed
in its light, and there was a faint smell of resin from their
wooden sides. The cry of an eagle echoed across the stillness.
Wu's murderer? This could be such a beautiful place, Wang
thought. No, it's man who makes it ugly, with our greed and
suspicion, and now with death itself.

11

The CAAC Antonov gave a lurch as it hit an air-pocket. A terrible grinding noise filled the cabin. Combat Hero Second Class Wang Anzhuang closed his eyes and said a prayer to Guan Di, God of War. "Don't let it happen . . ."

There were more bumps, more metallic groans, a sudden deceleration, a terrible revving of engines. The hero's last thoughts were of Mei and Zhengyi. Maybe this was for the best, after all. They could forget about him. Start a new life . . . The plane's canned *erhu* music went dead: the end would come in silence.

"This is Captain Yang. Thank you for flying CAAC."

Wang opened his eyes; they were taxiing across the tarmac.

"A most enjoyable flight," said Team-leader Chen, packing away a report from the Central Party Committee. "Most relaxing. Our national airline does a splendid job."

"So do our national railways," Wang muttered.

The Antonov came to a halt and a ladder was wheeled up to the side. The passengers began to disembark, each one recoiling as they stepped out into the tropical heat. By the time Wang reached the tarmac, he could feel his body tickling with sweat. And they still had to walk to the terminal . . . Then he heard a siren, and the outline of a car appeared in the haze. It acquired solidity, then colours—blue and white, police colours. It drew up right by them, and a smiling man in a check suit, bow tie and reflector sunglasses got out.

"Team-leader Chen Runfa?"

Chen nodded imperceptibly.

"Pao Xueyi." The man stuck out a hand. "Deputy Inspector, Customs Department. Welcome to the south!"

Chen grunted a reply; Pao Xueyi opened a rear door and coolness poured out of the vehicle like water. As the visitors got in, they sank into the seats.

"Not this warm up in Beijing then?" said Pao.

Chen remained silent.

"You'll get used to it," Pao went on. "Take it easy for a couple of days."

"We don't have time to take it easy," Chen snapped. "We've got work to do." He took out a file and buried himself in it.

They passed the airport gates. Wang peered through the window at the greenery fountaining up by the roadside. In the capital, it cost the government a fortune to keep the dust-red city alive with parks and trees. Down here, the battle seemed to be to stop nature running wild and devouring the streets and buildings. He found himself thinking that this lead couldn't have been much further from Huashan had it been deliberately planned.

"Can't you do something about this?" said Chen as the car tagged on to yet another traffic jam. "Restrict vehicle usage or something? This is ridiculous!"

Pao shrugged. "That's the way it is here. It's called prosperity."

"It's called anarchy. Put the siren on and get people to move out of our way! We're on state business!"

"No one would take any notice."

"*Ai-ya!*" said Chen, and went back to his file.

The 747 began its approach, so low over the roofs of Kowloon that Zhao could see people in swimming pools and detect makes of car in the streets. Mercedes. Porsche. Jaguar. The Beijing inspector had done this journey many times in his imagination, now it was for real. The West!

The plane touched down and the passengers disembarked

down a tube into the glass and concrete maze called Kai Tak airport. Zhao showed his badge to customs; standard procedure was followed and they waved him through. In arrivals, he was confronted by a line of people with names on boards. A fantasy came into his mind, that a plump young Chinese girl would be waiting for him in a leather mini-skirt and black stockings. And no knickers. She would sweep him off in a Rolls Royce to her flat on the peak, pour out two glasses of champagne . . .

A middle-aged Westerner with a drooping moustache was holding out a piece of cardboard with an approximation to the character "Zhao" on. He stuck out a blotchy, red-haired hand.

"Donald Fish. Inspector, Royal Hong Kong Police."

"Oh, er, Zhao. Zhao Heping. Pleased to meet you."

Fish nearly smiled. "Let me take your bag. You had a good journey?"

"Yes," Zhao lied: he'd been as nervous as Wang. "CAAC keep all their prettiest stewardesses for the international flights!"

Fish, a strict Presbyterian, grinned and started for the terminal door. Outside, a car was waiting. In the back was an interpreter from Xinhua News Agency, China's unofficial embassy in Hong Kong.

"I'm Ming Aimao," the interpreter said. Zhao shook his hand, wondering as he did so what this guy was doing here, as Fish seemed to speak passable Cantonese. The car sped off down a freeway lined with bright adverts in the old Chinese script.

Benetton. Stefanel. Häagen-Dazs.

"Capitalist exploitation," said Interpreter Ming.

Ah. Ming was here to keep an eye on him. Zhao made up his mind to escape from the guy as soon as possible. Meanwhile, the Westerner was trying to be friendly.

"This is our tunnel," said Fish, as the car disappeared into a tunnel.

Zhao nodded politely.

"This is Hong Kong island," said Fish, as the car re-emerged on Hong Kong island.

Another nod.

"And this is Wanchai."

Zhao's face lit up.

"A centre of bourgeois decadence," Interpreter Ming commented.

"What's that place?" Zhao asked, pointing at a doorway surrounded by pictures of half-naked women.

Fish grimaced. "That's the Golden Lotus Club. I'd stay away from there if I were you."

Interpreter Ming nodded.

"Is it expensive?" Zhao asked jokily.

"Everything is expensive in Wanchai," Fish replied. "Except the trams."

Zhao made a mental note to avoid the trams.

Deputy Inspector Pao Xueyi's office was an airy, white-walled room with a window that opened on to a garden of explosive purple bougainvillaea. An enormous propeller fan on the ceiling clanked round and round.

". . . We have no reason to suspect the smuggler was anything but a tourist," Pao was saying. "His name was Claude Bonnet, aged forty-five, from Paris, France—"

"I know where Paris is," Chen cut in.

"Of course. Bonnet has no previous convictions—we checked with Interpol. He was part of a tour group, on its way back out to Hong Kong. He bought the Buddha from a pedlar, for five hundred yuan—"

"How much?" said Wang.

"These tourists have money to burn."

"No, no. Those things are worth thousands and thousands of yuan in the West."

"I should like to question the smuggler," said Chen.

Pao shook his head. "That's, er, going to be difficult."

"Difficult?"

"Yes. He's gone home."

"He's what?"

"Gone home."

"This man is a key witness in a major police inquiry. And he's gone home? Where's your Unit Secretary? I want to speak to him at once."

"We consulted top officials in Beijing," Pao said nervously. "Avoid a diplomatic incident, they told us."

"I don't believe you."

"I can show you the documents."

"They couldn't have done. Knowing the seriousness of this investigation . . ."

Pao began rifling through his desk. He found the papers and handed them to Chen, who read them in silence.

"Wei signed this," the team-leader finally said. "Secretary Wei . . ." Then he gasped. "And Minister Tao." Then he went silent again. For a long while, there was only the noise of the fan and the traffic outside. A mosquito whined past Wang's ear, and he swatted it.

"Got to watch out for those buggers," said Pao, forcing a smile on to his face.

"Yes . . ." Wang replied. "So, er, you know where Bonnet brought the item, then?"

"Of course."

"What sort of place is it?"

"A street market."

"One with regular stallholders?"

"Yes."

"I think we should talk to these people. Don't you, Comrade Team-leader?"

Chen shook his head. "You go," he said, his voice a whisper.

Deputy Inspector Pao jumped to his feet. "I'll organize transport straight away!"

Wang and Pao, in a motorbike and sidecar, pulled off Sun Yat Sen Road into the alleyway.

"That's the place," said Pao. The bike nosed a path through the wall of shoppers and drew up at the kerb. The Cantonese customs official led Wang over to a stall festooned with day-glo nylon shirts.

"Kwok Man-ho," he said, pointing at the owner. "He saw Bonnet meet up with the vendor."

Kwok grinned and began jabbering in Cantonese. Pao translated. "He says he knew the guy was up to no good the moment he saw him."

Witnesses often had this second sight, even when observing perfectly innocent people. "What actually happened?" Wang asked.

More Cantonese.

"He says the guy stood on the corner, waiting for foreigners. When Bonnet came past, he stopped him. They talked. They disappeared. That's it."

"I'm sure that happens all the time in a big tourist city. Why report this to you?"

"We came round with a picture of Bonnet, asking if anyone had seen him. Several people had done. He had a pair of green trousers on. Really loud ones . . ."

Wang nodded. "Did this vendor talk to *every* foreigner?"

"No."

"Was there anything special about the ones he chose to stop?" Wang asked.

More Cantonese.

"They all seemed different. A bald man, a woman with blue hair, an old fellow with a stick."

"Hmm. And you got a tip-off, didn't you?"

"That's right. One of the hotel staff saw the Buddha in Bonnet's room. He could tell it was an antique, and reckoned the guy was going to try smuggling it out of the country."

"Could I speak to this fellow?"

"The tip was anonymous."

"Yes, of course . . . Have you interviewed all the staff?"

Pao looked surprised. "We have to respect informants' confidentiality."

"I understand." Wang paused. "This has been most useful." He turned to the stallholder. *"M-koi, Kwok Sin-shaang,"* he said: thank you, Mr. Kwok, in his best Cantonese. Which wasn't very good.

Kwok tried not to laugh.

"Find anything?" said Chen when they got back.

Wang shook his head. "Not really."

"Didn't think you would. These petty businessman types are most unreliable. You're lucky they didn't try and sell you some shoddy piece of rubbish made in Hong Kong."

Wang hid the kit-bag he had brought for Zhengyi behind his chair.

"Meanwhile," the team-leader went on, "I've been doing some work. I have a list here of all the major hotels. In the next few days, we will visit them and ask every single foreign tourist if they have seen any other artefacts from Huashan on sale. Sets of photographs are being faxed down tonight. I suggest starting with the biggest establishments and working downwards: you deal with the White Swan, I'll take the Liuhua. Any objections?"

"No . . ."

"It will be a lot of work, and we will need to be alert the whole time. There is a distinct possibility that some of these foreign tourists might in fact be agents. I suggest we turn in early, in preparation."

Their host looked disappointed. "If you want to see the city by night, I could show you around. It's quite an experience. I know a great karaoke bar, with some nice girls—"

"We have work to do tomorrow, Comrade Pao."

The local man glanced at Wang, who in turn looked at his boss.

"Maybe another evening."

Northerners!

The two Beijingers dined in the officers' canteen, at a table in a corner. Chen was silent the whole evening, except for a few disparaging comments about the cost of a banquet going on nearby: eleven senior policemen at a round table stacked high with food, getting louder and drunker as the evening went on.

Wang went to bed early—then lay awake, unable to sleep. The humidity! He got up and threw open the window. Noise came pouring in: car horns, bike bells, revving engines, music . . . He closed the window again, then realized he should never have opened it in the first place as the room was now full of insects. So he lay sweating under the bizarre gauze cone of his mosquito net, while various creatures fluttered and rattled against it. Surely one would find a way through . . . When he finally drifted off to sleep, he dreamt. The usual dream this time: massacre at Muxudi.

Zhao dined with Interpreter Ming in one of the Xinhua accommodation blocks.

"I envy you; returning home so soon," said Ming. "This is a foreign country in so many ways." He shook his head sadly. "The agency does its best to make us feel at home, but it's not easy . . ."

Zhao helped himself to another square of pork gristle and tried to look sympathetic. Around the walls were pastel landscapes of the homeland in traditional style, subtly evoking nostalgia, simplicity and patriotism. Zhao wanted to see bright lights, hear the latest, loudest music, taste novelty, strangeness, danger.

"I shall be lucky if I go back north before next Spring Festival," the interpreter went on. "There's nothing quite like Spring Festival in Zhengzhou, you know."

"I'm sure."

A tepid bowl of wonton soup followed, then a boiled sweet. Zhao pleaded tiredness.

"I think I'll have an early night."

"Good idea. Don't forget—if you can't sleep, there's a television room where we can get CCTV." Interpreter Ming shook his head. "The Hong Kong stuff is so vulgar."

Back in his room, Zhao checked the place for bugs. There didn't seem to be any, but just in case, he set his clock radio to play for an hour. He slid the window open with concentrated caution.

Perfect! A small ledge ran beneath each line of windows: a man of his skill and agility would have no problem edging along it as far as the vertical guttering. Then there was the outer wall, scanned by a closed-circuit camera mounted on the roof. The camera seemed fixed: assuming it had a regulation issue 35 mm lens, there would be a blindspot on the far left corner . . . Zhao retreated to take one last look in the mirror, smoothed back his hair, then climbed out into the hot tropical night.

Five minutes later, he was standing in the street. A taxi approached, its For Hire sign glowing like a beacon. Zhao flagged it down.

"Wanchai!" he told the driver.

12

Inspector Zhao made his way down the dimly-lit stairs of the Golden Lotus Club. A second bouncer at the foot asked him for more money.

"That was entrance up there. This is membership."

Despite his linguistic abilities, Zhao found this distinction too subtle to understand. However, the one thing he mustn't do was to kick up a fuss.

"Of course. How much?"

"Fifty dollars."

He stifled a groan and produced the money. He smiled at the thought of the journey back from Huashan, most of which he had spent persuading Chen how big a budget this Hong Kong mission would require.

By Western standards it was still early. The long chrome bar was deserted except for a dinner-jacketed barman cleaning glasses. Two girls in low-cut blouses, mini-skirts and black stockings stood in a corner, deep in conversation despite the synthesized disco music swirling around their ears. Were they wearing knickers? Would Zhao get a chance to find out?

Trying to look confident, he walked over to the bar. One of the girls looked up and flicked a glance at him. Some kind of signal?

Don't rush.

The barman approached. "Drink, sir?"

"I'll have a beer."

"The wine list is here, sir. I can recommend the Dom Perignon '66."

"Oh, thanks. I'll have a bottle—" He saw the price. *"Aiya!"* Zhao ran his finger up the price column till he found some stuff called Champagne Du Maison, which was only seventy-five dollars. He began taking out the cash.

"That's dollars US. It's four hundred HK."

The sum transformed itself into Chinese *renminbi*, into weeks worked, months of savings, years of rent. Zhao scowled, then counted out the money and handed it over.

"A waitress will bring it to your table, sir."

"Good." Zhao walked off and sat down in a comfortable corner. A few minutes later, a girl in a *qipao* split to the top of her thigh came over with two glasses and a substantial part of Zhao's budget bobbing in a huge silver cooler.

"Will you join me?" said the inspector, reaching for the bottle. The waitress smiled—her lacquer lipstick stayed shiny and unbroken even when her grin was at its broadest—then shook her head and strutted away. Zhao watched her go, then slowly poured himself a glass and raised it to nobody in particular.

"Ganbei!"

"Ganbei!"

Zhao spun round: a woman had taken the seat next to him. She was in her late thirties, her eyes heavy with mascara, her cheeks rouged and puffy.

"I'm Lily," she said. "Lily Wong. D'you mind if I join you?" When she smiled, little lines snaked out from the corners of her lips.

Zhao was about to say yes, he did mind—but he caught sight of the barman with a smirk on his face.

"No," he said instead. "Please do." He added an extravagant gesture of welcome as if Lily were exactly the companion he had been waiting for.

"Can I have a drink?" said Lily.

"Of course!" He poured one out. *"Ganbei!"* he said again.

"Ganbei!" The glasses clinked, and Zhao was suddenly overcome with pleasure. There was a glass of French cham-

pagne fizzing in his hand. Lily had put on delicious perfume, and was looking at him with deep brown eyes. An older woman would know more, understand more; the girls by the bar suddenly seemed shallow, jangling and cold.

"So, you're from—over there."

"You can tell that easily?"

"Your accent."

"Not the clothes?"

"No," Lily lied. She reached over and scraped a speck of dandruff off Zhao's shoulder.

"Well, I'm over here now—and I want to enjoy myself."

"You will. I'll make sure of that."

Zhao grinned. "Dancing!" he exclaimed suddenly. "I feel like dancing!"

"Ganbei!"

Lily raised her glass and gazed through the bubbles at the revolving silver ball in the ceiling. She was a little drunk by now.

"What's going to happen to us? After 1997, when you're in charge. When we're part of your People's Republic."

"Heaven knows," Zhao replied. "I guess things will be difficult—we're a puritanical lot."

Lily nodded, then took his hand. "Would you look after me? I've got a son, you see. Things would be difficult for him."

Zhao paused. "I'm not really important enough," he said eventually. "You should find yourself a nice Party Secretary. If there are any."

"I got myself an English boyfriend," said Lily. "Johnny, his name was. He bought me things, he took me to parties and clubs and shows just like I was an English girl. Of course, I was younger then . . ." Her face fell, then lit up. "D'you think I'd make a good Communist? I do believe the world should be more fair than it is. That's what Communism's supposed to be about, isn't it?"

Zhao frowned; Lily giggled.

"I'll tell you about the English!" she went on. "They're mad. They don't get any love when they're children, and they don't give their little ones any when they grow up. Johnny was thrown out of his home when he was eight years old and sent to a horrible school where he was beaten the whole time. Aged eight! If anyone laid a finger on my Walter—he's six now—I'd kill them!" Lily lowered her voice to a whisper. "We call it the 'English problem.' Lots of them suffer from it, especially the rich ones who went to those expensive schools. They can't make love unless you humiliate them first. Imagine that! I had to wear a mortar board and a gown, and spank poor Johnny on the bottom with a cane!" She giggled, put her arm round the inspector then waggled her empty glass.

"And where is he now?" Zhao asked.

"Still here. But he's married—properly, to an English girl. The Honourable Lavinia Lucas . . . You get used to that sort of thing as a hostess. You take what you can, while you can. And when you start feeling sorry for yourself, you go for a walk round Aberdeen harbour or go to Lantau and look at those transit camps. Then you fall down on your knees and thank the Lord for what you've got . . . Hey, that bottle's empty!"

"Well, er—"

Lily smiled and gave Zhao a hug. "You've only got one life, Comrade. You'll remember this, when you go back to boring old Beijing." She began to hum *The East is Red*, shaking her head from side to side and making the song sound particularly turgid.

Zhao called out: "Waitress!"

"Ganbei!"

Zhao looked at Lily again, and felt another rush of lust. They'd danced, they'd talked—time to move things on. But how? Had he misread her; was she just what she said, a hostess, who would take the suggestion of sex for money as an insult? No, that was absurd. Supposing he didn't have enough cash on him? If the cost of drinks here was anything to go by . . . He looked round at the other customers—from Hong Kong, Taiwan, Japan, America, Europe, India, Africa—and was consumed by envy of their worldliness. Only if there were a North Korean among them would there be someone with the same dismal, pompous, insular poverty as was expected of a citizen of the People's Republic.

Lily noticed his changed expression. "What's up?"

"Nothing. It's just . . ."

Lily crossed her legs, letting the *qipao* fall open to reveal even more thigh. Her stockings made a delicious fizzing sound.

"Do you want to make love?" she said.

"Yes. Of course I do. I've been—"

"So do I."

Zhao fumbled his glass, nearly tipping the contents over the erection that was bulging up under his badly-cut Terylene trousers.

"We'll talk money later," Lily went on. "There's a door to the back stairway by the stage."

Crossing the floor with her, Inspector Zhao felt like a million dollars. US.

Lily's room was small and functional; a skylight, a fan, a large mirror. She lit a joss-stick and sat Zhao down on the one chair; she ran her hand down into his crotch, then reached out for one of the erotic books on the bedside table.

"These are for Han visitors only," she said. "Foreigners don't understand. Their taste in love, as in everything else, is coarse."

Zhao took *Stories from the Imperial Palace* and began to read it. As he did so, he heard the sound of her dress unzipping.

"Choose a story to your liking," Lily said.

He let his eyes run over her half-naked body, then flicked back to the book. Each double-page had a drawing on one side, and a description in florid, literary Chinese on the other.

"Letting the bee make honey. The courtesan lies on her back, smoothing her hips with her hands and moving them gently from side to side. She raises her legs in the air; now the Emperor can see the lotus flower itself, and becomes as eager as a starving horse. But she is skilled in the art of love, and knows how delay heightens pleasure. She sits up and pushes him away, then runs one hand down his chest to his Jade Dagger . . ."

Zhao shivered with pleasure—something he had almost forgotten: back home, sex was a chore, a pretence, a keeping-up of face.

Lily was naked, now. She began to undress the Beijing policeman, whispering luscious obscenities in his ear, reaching down to his Jade Dagger and stroking it. He leant forward and buried his head between her breasts; he reached out for a nipple and savaged it with kisses—Lily let out a well-practised moan of pleasure, then pushed him gently away.

Letting the bee make honey. She slid back on to the bed, and began smoothing her hips with her hands . . .

In the headquarters of Xinhua News Agency, Interpreter Ming was having sweet dreams of his days in the Young Pioneers, sitting round a campfire singing revolutionary songs. Back in Zhengzhou, at Spring Festival.

Wang arrived at the White Swan Hotel early next morning. For a moment he stood and stared at the astounding display in the lobby—an enormous waterfall, plunging into a rockpool amid a mock jungle of exotic plants—then he disappeared into one of a line of soundproofed telephone booths. He dialled his office.

Constable Lu answered. "Hello, sir. It's nice to hear you. It's awfully boring here. How's things in Canton? It must be nice to—"

"There's a number I want you to investigate. Find out who it belongs to, and everything you can about the subscriber. And don't let them know you're on to them. If in doubt, stay in the background. Understand? Background. Especially if it's a private number and they have a beautiful daughter."

"Yes, sir."

"The number is 632-1275. Got it?"

Lu read the number back.

"Good. Don't try and contact me here. Just get the information. I'll ask you for it when I see you."

"Yes, sir."

The phone began to make a series of bleeping noises and cut Wang off.

The interviews were done individually, Wang confronting the nervous tourists with the pictures and asking if they had seen any of the artefacts on sale. So far, out of seventy-three, none had.

"Next, please."

A youngish overseas Chinese in chinos and a Lacoste T-shirt entered and announced himself as George P. Lim. Wang ticked him off the list. A fellow policeman, he noticed . . . The inspector uncovered the photographs, and watched Lim's eyes widen.

"Wow!"

Wang smiled: at last, someone who knew something about Chinese art.

"Tang dynasty, they must be," Lim went on. He spoke Mandarin, too. "The Golden Age of Chinese Culture." Wang smiled even more. "And they've been stolen? Maybe if you guys spent less time shooting students and more time guarding property—"

Wang's smile vanished. "I had nothing to do with Tiananmen," he snapped, though he was under strict instructions not to discuss politics.

"But you approve, I take it?"

"I'd hardly say if I didn't, would I?"

"No. I guess not . . ." Lim nodded thoughtfully, and looked slowly through the rest of the photos. "That's one hell of a haul," he said at the end. "Where did they come from?"

Wang was also under instructions to keep things moving. But he was fed up with gawping, shrugging, frightened tourists who didn't know the Tang dynasty from last Tuesday. He suddenly wanted to talk to this man, with whom, he felt, he might well have a great deal in common. "Trust no one": the words came back to him. But Lim was so far removed from this case that Wang knew he could make an exception.

"You really want to know?" he asked.

Lim nodded, and the inspector began to tell the story.

"So what do you make of it all?" Wang asked.

"Well. I don't know . . ." George Lim glanced around the room. "I'm sure you're right about that security guy, Wo. He's why you're here. But as to who his associates were . . . You've got so little to go on, that's the problem. Only that phone number—that might tell you something."

Wang suddenly wished he had entrusted its investigation to someone other than Constable Lu.

"But then it might not," Lim went on. "Either way, you're on your own." He grinned. "Still glad you became a cop?"

Wang laughed out loud. To have talked things over with a fellow professional was such a relief.

"Well, Anzhuang, if there's anything I can do to help you in your investigation, I'd really like to—"

Someone began knocking on the door. "Is everything all right in there?"

Lim scowled. "Hell, that's our tour guide. 'Empress Wu.' Get on the wrong side of her, and she'll make your holiday hell. It's been nice talking with you." The two men shook hands, and Lim headed for the door. As he grabbed the handle, however, he paused, then turned round.

"Why don't you join Amy and me for dinner tonight?"

Wang looked shocked. "I'm not sure if we're allowed—"

"If you want to do something badly enough, you do it. That's an American attitude. I recommend it. Seven o'clock, in the lobby."

Constable Lu stood in the street and swore. The rain was constant, and nobody had used the phone in the last half hour.

"I'll wait another ten minutes," he told himself.

Senior Party members get telephones free of charge; ordinary Chinese citizens have to pay for them. Several months' wages. To afford this luxury, many city dwellers set themselves up as public phone boxes. The most entrepreneurial become bureaux, making calls and taking messages for their customers. 632-1275 was one such outfit. Lu was now keeping their premises under surveillance, disguised as one of the thousands of itinerant bike-repair men in the capital.

"Five minutes . . ." he said as another rivulet of water wriggled down his back. A man appeared, wheeling a Flying Pigeon whose chain had come loose. After a short haggle over the cost of the repair, Lu got to work. He enjoyed mending things, and was so engrossed in his task that he missed the figure in a mac walk into the phone-bureau.

A note changed hands and a satisfied customer pedalled off into the rain. Lu wiped his hands on a cloth, tried to light a cigarette, toyed with the money in his pocket—then the man in the mac reappeared. His eyes were nervy and violent; Lu looked away at once, returning to his bicycle parts with relief. The man walked off. When his footsteps had died away, Lu peered after him. The desire to follow was overwhelming.

"He's up to no good," the young policeman told himself. But Inspector Wang had told him to be cautious. And then the figure was gone, anyway. If that had been Lu's golden opportunity to catch a villain, he had just missed it.

Wang found a bench under a palm tree and sat down. It was a lovely evening, warm and breezy. The Pearl River lapped by; old folk in Mao suits stood swaying through routines of *taijiquan*; two lovers sat hand in hand on a bench, staring out at the river.

If you want to do something badly enough, you do it. Easy to say, maybe, in America. But here in China . . . Still, he'd given Team-leader Chen the slip; he was looking forward to this meal. A ferryboat carved its way through the sparkling river water; music was playing from it. Life down south seemed easier, more open. What was it like even further south, across the border, in Hong Kong? It was a thought Wang had never allowed himself before.

The old ogres came into his mind. Those Holmes stories: the rich and the poor, unbridgeably divided. Capitalism as portrayed by the West's other great writers—Jack London, John Reed, Engels, Galsworthy. But they belonged to a bygone era; what was the West really like, now, in the 'nineties?

Out on the river, a wizened old man sploshed past, propelling his coal-lighter with a wooden oar. The eternal reality of Chinese life: *chi ku*, the bitterness of hard work. Wang's mind went back to Nanping village. All this talk of the West— wasn't this treachery? But down here in the warm, affluent south, the treachery seemed less. How much less?

A clock struck seven.

"Damn. Now I'm late. What will they think of me?"

George and Amy Lim were waiting in the hotel lobby, looking at a glass case of ginseng products "guaranteed to restore the male member to maximum power" and sharing a joke.

"Anzhuang, I want you to meet my wife."

Amy Lim, also a second-generation refugee from Mao's China, held out a soft, smooth hand to the Communist policeman. She was undoubtedly over thirty, but looked as young as a twenty-year-old mainlander. She smiled—mainland women either put on too much lipstick or none at all; Amy had it exactly right. As she had everything right—clothes, scent, above all a general demeanour of confident, lively femininity. In that moment, Wang understood exactly why those young students had looked outside the People's Republic for comparisons. And to do so didn't seem wrong at all.

"George has told me all about you," she said.

Wang stammered a reply. The three visitors walked out into the delicious balm of a tropical evening.

"I want to eat snake tonight," said George. "I believe there's a marvellous restaurant in town that serves nothing else."

Amy screwed up her face. "George!"

"Anzhuang, you like to eat snake, don't you?"

"I've never tried."

"Really? Then it's an adventure for all of us." He strode up to a taxi and shouted a command to the driver. "By the way, everything's on me tonight," he added as they got in. Wang shook his head, George insisted, Wang refused—the taxi left the island and began to wind its way up the back alleys of the great southern city.

The Snake Restaurant was full of Chinese businessmen shouting into mobile phones and Western tourists giggling at the items on the menu. Snake with cat! The new arrivals were shown to a private room where they could be charged extra. Wang noticed a microphone by the ventilator, but doubted very much it was still in regular use. Besides, they'd agreed in the taxi: no politics.

"You're coming to Beijing, I trust," said Wang. He'd take them to the Wild Goose Mansion for Beijing *jiaozi* dumplings, or the *Quanjude* for duck, or Ji's for roasts . . .

"Oh yes," George replied. "Staying at—where is it? The Kangxi Hotel?" Amy nodded. "You know it, Anzhuang?"

"Yes," said Wang. It was right next to the Qianlong, the hotel where Jasmine had sung—and where Wang had once reckoned he could infiltrate a Triad operation. Some hope! A feeling of dejection came over him, at the thought of her guilt, at the thought of the unearned, unworthy praise that had come his way at his solution of Xun Yaochang's murder.

George Lim poured out a glass of *Maotai* and handed it to Wang.

"*Ganbei!*" said the American, and downed it in one.

Amy Lim did the same.

Wang hesitated. Come on, he told himself—get into the party mood!

"*Ganbei!*" The clear, powerful spirit seared down his throat.

Drink and sing. How long is life?

13

The end of the week. Constable Lu hadn't much to report. Lots of faces, most of whom he'd forgotten; one or two regulars on whom he'd made notes. And the man in the mac, whose eyes he would never forget. He had also become adept at mending bicycles, won a fight with another repairman who reckoned Lu was trying to muscle in on his patch, and earned more in a week than a police constable earned in a month. He had just fixed a puncture—another one yuan fifty—when he looked up and saw the man again. Or rather, the mac.

Don't let him see your face!

Lu began tidying his toolkit. The man splashed past—it had rained every day of the surveillance operation—and entered the telephone bureau. Lu's pulse began to race; a wrench fell from his grasp with a deafening clatter.

Keep calm.

The man seemed to take an age to come out: when he did, he walked off in a hurry, not even glancing at the twitching cycle repair-man opposite. He disappeared round the corner.

"Now!" said the young constable. "I have to!"

"No . . ." a voice inside told him—but he had already packed his tools into the pannier and was wheeling his bike down the *hutong*.

Remember what they taught you at Police College. Keep your distance. Merge in with the crowd.

Lu nearly lost his quarry several times, but when the young constable emerged on to Chongwen Street, there he was, talking to a rickshaw driver. Haggling? Yes: he got in and the pedal-powered vehicle creaked off. Lu followed slowly up the rain-soaked bike lane, always extra careful, always pacing himself to look natural but never losing sight of the rickshaw. It turned into Zhan-xi, jinked past the International Hotel, swung down on to the capital's new ring road. With each turn, Lu felt his pulse quicken. Follow your intuition, Inspector Wang always said.

The Kangxi Hotel came into view. Then the Qianlong. Constable Lu stifled a cry of astonished excitement as the rickshaw turned into the second of the two driveways.

The plane from Canton touched down at about six-thirty. A car was ready to meet Chen.

"I'd offer you a lift, Wang, only it's not really in my direction," said the team-leader. "See you tomorrow morning . . ."

Wang was quite happy to take a bus. As it bumped back into town, he tried to get comfortable on the plastic seat and gazed out at the stony landscape with its hardy thorn trees and short spiky grass. It might not be lush, but it was home.

Back at Flat 1008, Wang went straight to the kitchen and prepared himself a northern-style meal—one with a decent amount of spices and with noodles, not rice. He put on a cassette of Beijing Opera and sat sipping green tea on his little balcony looking out over the rain-bright roofs of the capital. His home.

The south was already just a memory; its temptations, its dreams, its unreality. Wang was a northerner, Shandong-born like Confucius. He was (or had been until the ritualistic mass-"resignations" caused by the recent campaign) a Party member . . . Perhaps he'd been a bit unwise, going out for that dinner with an American couple. Perhaps he ought to renege on his promise to meet them when they came north. He had several days to concoct a decent excuse; if George understood China as well as he seemed to, he would realize why.

Thus reassimilated into his home environment, Wang sat down and began some good old-fashioned *qigong* exercises. Let those thoughts go—all of them. Just breathe. In, out . . .

R-ring!

The inspector stifled a curse and walked over to the phone.

"Yes," he snapped.

"Oh, hello, sir. It's Lu here."

"What d'you want?"

"Could we meet? It's important . . ."

They met under Zhengyang Gate, as before. Lu told his story: Wang listened in silence. At the end, the inspector said nothing.

Lu looked worried. "I did do the right thing, sir, didn't I?"

Wang glanced up. "Not according to the rule book. But yes, of course you did." He clapped the young lad on the shoulder.

"Thank you, sir."

"We mustn't jump to conclusions, that's all. We don't know the character you followed was anything to do with the Huashan thieves—simply that he looked shifty and used the same telephone bureau. If that place has one lot of crooked clients, it might have several."

Lu nodded. "But it's a coincidence, don't you agree?"

"Yes."

"And you're always saying how you don't believe in coincidences."

"Yes . . ." Wang stared down at the ground, lost in thought. Then he straightened up. "Lu, you mustn't mention any of this to anyone. Team-leader Chen, Secretary Wei . . . You've done well, extremely well. But now you must keep quiet. Totally quiet. 'Disaster begins with an open mouth,' remember."

"Yes, sir," said Lu.

"I knew I was right to trust that job to you."

Wang pedalled slowly home. He put his bike in the rack and locked it, summoned the lift, cursed—the lift shut off at nine-thirty—and walked slowly up the stairs. Back in Flat 1008, he crossed to his writing desk, and sat down.

Be scientific, he told himself.

He took a sheet of paper, and began to scribble on it. In the centre he put the Qianlong Hotel. Radiating out from it were boxes, filled with names, dates, events. In a corner he wrote Huashan. Then he linked that up to the hotel: a line from the Goddess of Mercy to the Yi Guan Dao? Why not? Of course! He crossed a line out and drew another one. Then another . . .

It was nearly midnight by the time he had produced a diagram that fitted all the known facts. His wastebin was full of crumpled papers: theories that had nearly worked but not quite. Tomorrow he would burn them: the Triad mustn't have a chance of guessing how his mind was working. The inspector sat and stared at his handiwork. Part of him—the young man who had led a charge in Vietnam—knew it was right, and wanted to act on it at once. An older, more experienced Wang reckoned it was an interesting hypothesis.

Sleep on it, he told himself. Then he had a better idea. Wang picked up the piano stool and carried it over to his bookshelf. Standing on the stool, he could just reach the top, where his fingers found a dusty cardboard box and what looked like a bolt of material. He lifted them down with a strange reverence, as if they were alive, and placed them on his writing table.

A little, half-conscious glance round, a firm pulling-to of the curtains, and Wang began to unwrap the material. Inside was a book. He opened the box and took out a bundle of yarrow stalks, two small incense jars and some joss-sticks. He set them up, the book between the jars, facing due south, the stalks beside it . . .

In Nanping village, Granny Peng had spent many afternoons filling the head of her bright, inquisitive young grandson with Chinese folklore. Geomancy, Taoism, medicinal herbs, legends (his favourites had been about Bao Gong, a magistrate who protected the poor from injustice)—and, of course, the *I Ching*. Wang could see her now, unwrapping the yellowing text as she explained in a hushed voice how the Ancients had understood the nature of fate. "*Yin* and *Yang* are always changing in heaven," she would say, taking down the yarrow divining sticks and laying them out on the table. "Human affairs follow them." She would kowtow, light the incense, mumble a prayer . . .

Wang lit the joss-sticks. "Of course, I don't really believe it, the way Granny did," he told himself. "It's just a tool, a way of concentrating the mind."

The old lady had kowtowed to the book, kneeling before it and tapping her forehead on the floor. Wang didn't feel it was modern to do that. He bowed respectfully instead. The smoke from the sticks began to spiral a clear, grey path to the ceiling. She had said this was a signal to the ancestors. Her grandson didn't believe this, of course—but still broke the smoke-path three times with the yarrow sticks, exactly as she had done.

"It's worked in the past. After all, what was it Deng Xiaoping said: 'It doesn't matter if the cat is black or white, as long as it catches mice'?"

The divination began.

Wang had once tried to explain the method to a foreigner. You build up a hexagram of six lines, which are either broken—*Yin*—or solid—*Yang*. Lines are determined by random divisions of the yarrow stalks and a counting of sub-groups off against one another—different remainders generate different lines. There are sixty-four possible hexagrams: further permutations are created by the existence of static and moving lines . . . The foreigner had stopped him halfway through: an earnest rationalist from a European far-left group, she had then begun to question his interest in feudal practices. Typical Westerner, patronizing and ill-informed . . .

Three divisions and three counts yielded the bottom line—a broken one, showing the force of *Yang* to be in the ascendant. A good start. Two more lines produced the bottom trigram: thunder. The pattern began to repeat itself—another *Yang*, another *Yin* . . . Wang prepared himself for the last division of the yarrow stalks.

"Think of nothing but the problem," Granny Peng would say. "The ancestors hear even unspoken words." Who heard now, in 1991? Marx? Mao? Wang's eyes wandered to the old family photograph on the dresser. Listen now. Please.

He made the last division, counted the stalks and calculated the outcome. A second thunder trigram, making the whole hexagram number fifty-one. *Zhen*, double thunder, explosive action.

Wang knew the main commentaries, those of Confucius and King Wen the Wise. They would be counselling that immediate action was the only solution to the problem in hand. To hesitate would be to court disaster. Attack leads to victory; waiting for the enemy's next move is fatal.

Wang put the paraphernalia back in its box, wrapped the sacred book in its cloth, and put them all back in their special high place.

The inspector was unusually silent on the drive out to Hu-ashan. Zhao told Team-leader Chen all the clues and leads he had discovered in Hong Kong.

"I must have met every policeman and every informer in the colony," he said. "None of them knew anything."

"You certainly spent enough money..." Chen commented.

Zhao shrugged. "I said it was an expensive place. I was right. Nothing comes cheap: least of all information."

"But we haven't got any information."

"We know those artefacts aren't going through Hong Kong or Macao."

"Then what the hell was that Buddha doing in Canton?"

"I don't know," Zhao replied, suddenly looking dejected. "The only explanation I can come up with is that it was, deliberate. Some kind of diversion. There's probably a boat-load of the bloody things heading for Taiwan right now."

Wang smiled. Just what he reckoned. He was about to say so, but Chen spoke first.

"We certainly didn't find too much in Canton. And I was appalled by the laxity of our colleagues down there, both ideo-logically and professionally. I got the distinct impression that Deputy Inspector Pao Xueyi would do anything for money." He paused. "And yet much of our Revolution was created in the south. I can't help feeling that whole part of the country has succumbed to what Chairman Mao referred to as 'sugar-coated bullets.' Bourgeois comforts, cultural frivolity, foreign ideology."

Chen began reeling off a speech; by the end, Wang's en-thusiasm for sharing his feelings about the Canton Buddha had waned. Trust no one: that had to be his motto. A few more miles, and the car turned off metalled road on to the track that led up the Huashan valley, first through a pine forest, then across open rock. They reached the compound; Constable Tang, promoted to driver for the day, hooted the horn. As usual, nobody came out to let them in.

Wang sat in Cave One, panting like an old man.

"You shouldn't have attempted the climb this time of day," said Fen, now formally appointed Chief Security Officer. "It's summer now. I'm not having people up here keeling over with heat stroke."

"No . . ." Wang replied. But he had been so keen to get moving.

"I'm tightening up all round," Fen went on. "Safety and security. I'm determined to catch this thief."

Wang waited till his pulse was nearly normal, then left the cave. He walked slowly up the path, making a short detour into Cave Twenty-two to admire the wall paintings again. The City of Willows—the Buddhist heaven; the safety of the Triad lodge. Linked, possibly, after all . . .

At the top of the site, he found two guards playing Chinese chess. They let him pass without demur.

It did not take long to reach the point from which Wu had fallen. Wang lifted the bunting and stood staring down at the cracked lip of the path. Why? The question came back to him, as fresh as when he left a week ago.

Now, perhaps, he knew. He lay face-down on the pathway, spreading his weight as evenly as possible. Then he reached over the side of the ledge and began groping around with his hand. Nothing. He would have to lean right over the edge. The thought filled him with fear, but he had no option. He wedged his feet into a crevice and slowly spun himself round, so that his torso was hanging over the edge of the abyss. For an instant, a terrible dizziness overcame him. An image spun into his mind: Wu's thigh-bone, jutting through the dead man's stomach. Wang sat up, took ten deep breaths, then leant out over the edge again.

He found the crevice easily. It was tiny, but big enough to get a hand into. Nothing. Then his fingers brushed something hard and shiny. A scorpion clattered out of the crevice and vanished across the rockface. Wang paused again—did it have a partner?—then resumed his search.

"Ah!" Again, something smooth. And this time, inanimate.

Wang's spirits soared. He'd guessed right. He gripped the object and pulled at it. It came easily.

A moment later, the inspector was sitting on the pathway, looking at a stoneware plate with a rich bottle-green glaze. It wasn't quite in the class of the missing Guanyin, but the latest Huashan theft—number fifty-six, incident date last Thursday— was still a thing of great beauty.

14

Wang had brought a meal with him. He sat on the pathway, eating it; when he had finished, he threw the chicken bones and orange peel out over the precipice and watched them curl away into the valley below. Then he wrapped the stolen plate in the plastic bags that had contained the food and set off for the camp. As easy as that.

He took his time on the way down: a game of chess with the guards by the outcrop, a necessary visit to the latrine, a brief pilgrimage to Cave Twenty-two. He was just passing Cave One—

"Comrade Wang!"

It was Fen.

"A moment, if you please. We're carrying out random searches of personnel nowadays. I must ask you to hand that bag over."

Two guards came out and joined them.

"Tu, body-search the inspector." Fen took Wang's lunch-pack and began checking the contents. "Liao, make a note of these. Flask, one, empty. Notebook, one. Pen, one." Fen turned the pack upside down, shook it, crumpled it, waved it around his head—then handed it back. Tu ran his hands over the inspector's body, checking pockets, Wang's holster, even trouser turn-ups.

"Nothing here, sir."

"Your men are thorough," Wang commented. "I congratulate you."

Fen smiled. "Sorry to have bothered you, Comrade Inspector."

Late in the afternoon, the site latrines were emptied. Wang watched as a barrel of chemicals and excrement was lowered down the hoist and carried by the most junior porters to a cesspit, where it was emptied, upturned, swabbed out and left to dry in the hot summer sun. The pit was some way from the camp, and hidden from it by a ridge of rock and a copse of pine trees.

"Quite right, too," Wang said to himself as he crossed the ridge and was hit by the stench.

"Imagine you're the thief," he added, flicking away the cloud of flies that came to greet him. "And think of the millions of night-soil collectors who spread this stuff on the fields day in, day out. Shit-shovellers: that sergeant put it so well. For them, it's survival. For the Yi Guan Dao, it's millions of yuan."

He took a stick, and, fighting back rising nausea, began poking around in the cesspit. It did not take him long to find the plate—still wrapped in those plastic lunch-bags. He hauled it out and gave it a very good slooshing from the hose kept there to clean the vats; he took a pair of tongs from his pocket and removed the plate from its protective coats. It was undamaged and untarnished. And safely off the mountain.

Wang took the plastic away and buried it by the trees, then returned to his office with the plate under his jacket. The next task, of course, was to get it to Beijing. But that was easy. Take it. The VW Shanghai was only given a routine check when it left the camp—one which never extended to the briefcases, files and boxes in its boot. No doubt the same applied to other senior officials' vehicles.

One last thing: a call to the Kangxi Hotel.

"Yes, Lim. George P. Lim. From California . . . He has arrived? Good. Can I speak to him?"

•   •   •

It was a perfect summer weekend evening in Temple of Heaven Park. Golden sun filtered through the cypress trees; gentle music wafted out of the park loudspeakers; kites bobbed in a clear blue sky. An old man in a Mao suit sat playing folk tunes on an *erhu*.

The dust and paranoia of Huashan seemed a million miles away. Wang walked slowly along the pathway till he found a bench with a view of the Qinian Hall, the most beautiful building in China (and thus, obviously, in the whole world); he sat and stared at the three azure roofs rocketing up into the sky. Perfection.

"Anzhuang!"

Lim was alone and on time.

"George! Good to see you. Did you enjoy Suzhou?"

"Enjoy? I loved it. Those gardens! That's what being Chinese is all about . . ."

Retirement to a world of classical beauty, to drink wine and read the classics in a moonlit, waterside pavilion . . . To dream about those things was to be Chinese. In reality? *Chi ku*, to "eat bitterness," to do your share of shit-shovelling.

"I need your help," said Wang.

"With the case?"

"Yes."

The American smiled. "As long as there's no trouble."

"There won't be—for you. It's quite simple . . ."

George Lim walked into the gift shop of the Qianlong Hotel and browsed around. The assistant, a cadre's son devoid of interest in the retail or hotel trade, took no notice, only looking up from his soft porn magazine when George addressed him directly.

"Have you got anything better?" the American asked, pointing to the pottery section.

The young man shook his head. Bloody overseas Chinese— never satisfied.

"I'm looking for sculpture," George went on. "Really nice stuff. I'm prepared to pay," he added, slapping two fifty-yuan Foreign Exchange Certificates on to the table.

The boy put his magazine down and made a grab for the notes. George snatched them back.

"I want the best. I'll be discreet."

The boy looked him up and down. No, he wasn't a government agent. Nobody from the People's Republic, not even his mates, could wear quite such expensive clothes in quite such a slapdash way.

"Give me the money," he said, "and I'll introduce you to someone who'll sell you what you want."

George held out one of the notes. "You get the rest on satisfactory completion of purchase."

"Be back here in an hour."

George did as he was told, to the minute. He was greeted with a smile from a small fat man in a Western suit.

"If you'd like to come this way, sir . . ." The man led the way down a corridor and into an office. He offered George a padded leather chair and sat down at a desk. A third person sat watching the proceedings, his chin buried in his hands, a malevolent glare emanating from his eyes. The American policeman had encountered plenty of individuals like this on the streets of San Francisco; bodyguards to senior gangland figures.

"I want good art," George began. "And I want it old. Tang dynasty, if possible."

The small man nodded. "You are, of course, aware that there is an export prohibition on any item more than a hundred years old."

"I know. A guy was busted for it when I was down in Canton." Wang had asked him to mention this, and to see how the man reacted: the fellow remained ice-cool. "I'm prepared to run the risk," George continued. "The Tang is the golden era for me. Of art, of poetry, of sculpture . . . You only have one life, so why not have the best?"

"Very true. But what makes you think you can get items of that quality here? You're not on our hotel register."

George shrugged. "I'm staying at the Kangxi. They didn't have anything I liked."

The man smiled. He knew George was telling the truth; he'd checked with his opposite number at the neighbouring hotel. He stood up, walked across to a drawer and took out several pieces of *Sancai* pottery, a vase, a silver plate . . .

"How much is the warrior?"

"Twenty thousand."

"Yuan?"

The man scowled. "Dollars. If you want quality, you have to pay for it."

"Yes, but . . ."

The man packed all the goods away. A second, lower drawer contained inferior works. "What about that?" George asked, pointing to a rough-cast bronze of a galloping horse.

The vendor looked at his client with contempt. But not suspicion. "It's six hundred. You want to examine it?"

"Yes, please."

George took it and held it. It was a fake, but an old fake: antique collecting had become popular as early as the Ming dynasty, so forgery had, too. This was as near as an honest sergeant in the SFPD was likely to get to owning a genuine Tang artefact.

Back in his room, George put the statue on his dressing table and stared at it. Western artists had had to wait for photography before they understood the mechanics of the gallop. His Chinese ancestors had known two thousand years earlier.

I'm so glad we came back, he said to himself, then packed the piece away in his suitcase, together with the introductory letter from Anzhuang to Deputy Inspector Pao Xueyi, Customs Dept., Canton. Fifty dollars, the inspector had said, should be more than enough.

At a quarter-to four, he set out for the city centre. As he walked out of the front door, he noticed a man following him. He'd been expecting this: all he had to do was give the guy the slip. No confrontation. George took a taxi to the Forbidden City: a second taxi followed. He joined the queue for foreigners: the tail tried to join him and was shunted on to the queue for mainland Chinese by a steward.

"I'll pay the extra!" the tail protested, but the official was adamant. The Chinese queue was longer, and could not be jumped. Even the offer of money had no effect on the steward: the tail had come up against that most priceless of pearls, an honest official. George Lim didn't even look back as he headed down the long tunnel into the great Imperial Palace.

•   •   •

Wang's directions had been excellent; George had no problem finding the public telephone in the *hutongs* northeast of the Forbidden City exit. He knocked on the grimy wooden door, and an old woman led him through a rubbish-filled courtyard into a neat living room, where a group of people were sitting on a sofa.

"Join the queue," she said, pointing to the floor. "Do you want a mug of tea?"

"Oh, thank you."

"That'll be twenty fen."

The other customers, alerted by his clothes and his accent, crowded round him. "Are you American?" was their first question; when he said yes, they began bombarding him with queries about life in the States. When the current caller finished, they insisted he go next so they could all listen to his conversation.

"Please, this is private," he protested, which only made them listen harder. He dialled and got through.

"Hello, Anzhuang? Good . . . Yes, I did everything you wanted. No. Well, it's not very easy to talk. I've got an audience."

Wang, at the other end, laughed. "It's still safer than calling from those hotels," he said. "So, tell me what the fellow looked like."

"Short, fat, Western suit. Rings on his fingers. In his thirties, I'd guess."

Wang looked through the dossier of photographs he had been preparing all day. "Square sort of chin?"

"Yeah."

"Puffy eyes?"

"That's the guy. I don't know his name, I'm afraid."

"That's OK. I do. It's Li. Li Dehong. What were the pieces on offer like?"

"Lovely. He knows his trade. But I didn't recognize anything of yours."

"No, you wouldn't. Those would be extra, extra special, for export only. I hope you got yourself something nice."

"I did."

"Pao Xueyi will look after you. Any reaction from Li when you mentioned Canton?"

"No."

"Ah. Never mind."

"He's a cool customer."

"Yes . . . Tell me about the room: access, contents, layout." George did so.

"And was Li alone?"

"No. He had a bodyguard. A guy who just sat in the corner, watching. Big, mean-looking."

"Any distinguishing marks?"

George thought of the man, sitting and staring. "Didn't see any."

"Fine. And that statue I mentioned. Buddha Maitreya, southern Song dynasty."

"No sign of it."

"Ah, well. Were you followed?"

"Yes."

"I'm sorry about that. They may keep an eye on you for another day or so, till they get bored with all the tourist sites. I'm afraid it means we can't really meet up."

"I guessed that. You'll just have to come to the USA instead."

"Yes . . ." Wang replied. The idea, which would have been anathema a few years ago, suddenly seemed most attractive. "Anything else worth mentioning?"

"Don't think so."

"Thanks for everything, George. You've done me a huge favour." The two policemen said their goodbyes, Wang sent wistful best wishes to Amy, then the conversation was over.

That evening, Wang took his diagram out of the false-bottomed drawer where he had concealed it, scrubbed out a dotted line and replaced it with a clear, strong one.

15

The door of the cell creaked open. Jasmine Ren glanced up from the corner where she now spent most of the day in a silent huddle. Instead of leaping to her feet and attacking the new arrival, she just turned her head and muttered: "Oh, it's you."

"That's right."

The warder pulled up the cell's one chair for the visitor to sit on. Wang ignored him and squatted down on the floor.

"Leave us, please, warder. And close the shutter and turn off the intercom."

"Sir, I think—"

"Do as I say."

The warder gave a shrug and went out.

"Trying to be nice?" said Jasmine. "Trying to win me over with a little display of trust? Or have you got something nastier in mind? I wouldn't put it past you dogs . . ."

"I want to talk in private, that's all."

"I've got nothing new to say. How many more times do I have to say it? I stuck that knife in Xun Yaochang's neck—"

Wang leant forward. "Show me where, exactly."

"D'you really want me to?"

"Yes. Why not?" Wang stretched forward a bit more. "The

precise spot: that killer knew what he was doing.''

Jasmine paused then jabbed her finger into Wang's neck: the inspector gritted his teeth with pain.

''I'm glad that hurt,'' she said.

''It didn't,'' he lied. ''And it wasn't anywhere near where Xun was stabbed.'' Which was the truth. ''I think it's time you retracted that fake confession of yours and told me the truth. Let's start—''

''*Go to hell!* I've said I did it. What more d'you want? I hated the cheating bastard. He deserved it. And I'm not playing any more of your silly games—''

''I can get your father released.''

Jasmine Ren fell silent.

''He's been kidnapped, hasn't he?'' Wang went on. ''By the people stealing those statues.''

''I don't know anything about statues,'' Jasmine said slowly. ''Is that what all this is about? Dad's collection?''

Wang paused. She really didn't know? ''If you want to help him, you must help me. I imagine the kidnappers have said that they'll kill him if you drop your story. You've got to play along, even go to jail; they say they'll come and rescue you when it's all clear.''

Jasmine tried to keep an expressionless face.

''You've got to understand that these people are ruthless,'' Wang continued. ''There's no guarantee that they'll keep their side of the bargain. None at all. They're more likely to kill your father and let you rot in jail. D'you see that?''

''How d'you know all this?''

''It's my business to know things. I'm a policeman.''

''Who came snooping round our home setting up some phoney business deal . . .''

''That was a routine undercover investigation. When we get your father released, you'll be glad we undertook it.''

''And how do I know you're not at it again? More lies, more deception—''

''You don't know. You have to choose to trust me.''

The singer stared at Wang for what seemed like an eternity.

''Why are you doing this? What's in it for you?''

''You're accused of a crime you didn't commit. I happen to believe in a thing called justice.''

Jasmine burst out laughing. "Which is why you joined the bloody police!"

"Exactly."

She fell silent again.

Then sighed. "What d'you want me to do?"

"Talk to me. Be honest."

Jasmine looked round at the walls of the cell. "What d'you want to know?"

"First, tell me about the Qianlong Hotel."

"The Qianlong?"

"Yes. Tell me how you got the job there."

The look of puzzlement on her face had to be genuine. "There was an audition . . ."

"Your father had no part in getting you that job?"

"No. Certainly not. It was on merit." Pride flickered back into her eyes.

"You're sure of that?"

"Absolutely."

"Did your father know anyone who worked there? Think. This could be important."

"No. Well, no one apart from Li."

Wang remained expressionless. "Li?"

"The guy in charge of entertainment—he's got some fancy title . . ."

Wang resisted the temptation to fill the gap.

"My dad told me to watch out for him," Jasmine went on, " 'cause he was a bit of a womanizer. So I did. I'm afraid I can't tell you much about him."

"Can you tell me anything at all?"

"Not really . . . Is he involved in all this?"

"Possibly."

"I'll kill him if he is."

"You'll need to be out of prison to do that. And I'd stick to the law if I were you. You really know nothing about Li?"

"No. Well, he's quite a big shot. My dad said he could protect me from most people, but not Li." Jasmine looked regretful. "I told him I didn't need protection . . ."

"We all need a bit of help from time to time," said Wang. "Now, tell me about some of the people you *did* come into contact with at the Qianlong."

"Well, there was the barman, Sheng. Not much to say about him: he kept himself to himself. And there was poor old Eddie. Zheng Kangmei, the floor manager. I'm afraid he fell head over heels in love with me. I can't say I felt the same. Nice guy, but weak—inside, I mean, not just physically. Then there's the guys in the band . . ." She shook her head. "They must think I'm real scum, letting them down like this. We were going places."

"You still could if I can get you out of this place. Anyone else?"

"Not really. I just got on with my music."

"Right. Does the name Luo mean anything to you? Or Pang?"

Jasmine looked puzzled again. "Luo Pang is a business colleague of my dad's. I don't think he's got anything to do with the Qianlong."

"Tell me about him."

"I don't know anything. It's just a name I've heard. He's important, I know that."

"How?"

"Dad always said: 'If Luo Pang calls, interrupt me, whatever I'm doing.' But he never did call, not while I was around, anyway. Is he part of this, too?"

"No. Maybe. I'm not even sure he exists."

"He exists all right. I remember names."

A codename, then, probably. A 'Luo Pang' call would be on Triad business.

Wang offered Jasmine a Panda and lit one himself. Last one in the packet. Fine. "Now, if you don't mind, I'd like to talk a bit about Xun."

"Do we have to?"

"Yes. The obvious question first: do you have any idea who did kill him?"

"No. Xun said there were guys after him. He said he had information about them, and was going to get money for it. At the time, I thought it was very daring." She puckered her face in self-disgust.

"Did you tell your father about this?"

"Oh, no. Xun had sworn me to secrecy. Then when he went off, I felt too ashamed to talk about it."

"And you have no idea who these people were?"

"No."

"And you never asked?"

"Dad taught me never to meddle in other people's business."

"Including his own?"

"That's right."

Wang nodded. "You and Xun did go to the opera together, didn't you?"

"Yes. Several times. It's what attracted me to him, actually. A lot of Dad's friends had, well, unsophisticated tastes. Xun was different—on the surface. I didn't understand then how disgusting people can like beautiful things."

"But you didn't go on the night of the murder?"

"Oh, no. We'd split up; I wouldn't be seen dead with him."

"No . . . Any idea who he might have been going there to meet?"

Jasmine shook her head.

"Did Xun ever introduce you to any of his business associates?"

"Oh, no. Like I said, he wanted that part of his life separate."

"And he never mentioned Triads at all?"

Jasmine's look of shock was real. "He was involved with them?" She laughed. "Serve him bloody right!"

Wang pulled an envelope out of his pocket. "Now I want you to look at some photographs. If you recognize any of them, tell me. And if possible, when and where you have met them."

He laid a series of mug shots on the floor of the cell. One by one, everyone who worked at Huashan. Even his own colleagues.

"Remember, both your father's life and your own are threatened by people he regarded as friends. Neither you nor he owe a scrap of loyalty to any of them."

"No . . ." Jasmine ran her eyes over the gallery of faces. "That's your pal, isn't it? The young lad who came to one of my shows."

"Quite right. You'd not seen him before, I take it."

"Only when he came snooping round my father's. With you."

"Anyone else you know?"

Jasmine shook her head. "Sorry." Then she pointed at a picture of Team-leader Chen. "Who's that one?"

Wang felt a shiver of excitement. And fear. Chen!

"Why d'you ask?"

"He's ugly."

"But you don't know him?"

"No. Never seen him before. Or any other of these people, apart from your youngster."

Wang let the pictures lie there a while—how dare you accuse us, their eyes seemed to say. Then he gathered them up and packed them away. It had been a long shot. Its failure hadn't proved a thing.

"Now, if I'm to help you, Jasmine, you'll have to carry on your act. You've confessed; our talk was a waste of time—"

The young singer's face lost its new-found sparkle at once. "I can't go on for ever. D'you know what it's like, waiting to die?"

"Yes. One day I'll tell you about it, if you're interested in old soldiers' stories. Right now, you must have courage. And trust." He looked her straight in the face.

"Trust . . ." she replied hesitantly.

Wang kept on looking. Trust. He turned away. "One thing: if you hear that I have been killed, you can stop the act. Go and plead with the Prosecutor; tell him everything; get yourself freed."

"And my father?"

"His kidnappers won't stick to any bargain. You'll be more help to him outside than in here."

"Tell me who they are!"

"I can't."

"If I'm supposed to trust you—"

"I don't know who they are," Wang replied. "Not for certain. When I do know for certain, I shall act. Like double thunder," he added, tracing the hexagram *Zhen* on his palm.

Wang returned to his office and sat at his desk, shuffling the photographs like a pack of cards. He laid them out on the table. Such innocent-looking faces.

Dr. Jian.

Professor Qiao. No, not Qiao.

Hei Shou, the Party man.

His own team; Chen, Zhao and Fang (why had Fang volunteered to stay on at Huashan?).

A supporting cast: Wu's deputy, Fen; the hoist operator, Zhang . . .

"A trap," Wang said to himself. "That's the fairest way. The only way to be certain."

He sat back in his chair. A quote from Sun Tzu came into his mind. Yes, that would work nicely. First, he had to—

Someone was knocking at the door.

"Come in!" Wang's voice was cheerful, eager, alive.

Team-leader Chen entered. "Are you ready, Comrade?"

"Ready? What for?"

"Political Study, of course. You didn't forget, did you?"

"No. Of course not."

"It's going to be an old-fashioned Struggle Session. The Unit Committee will be looking at our self-criticisms again. With great thoroughness," Chen added with a smugness born of knowing that other people's self-criticisms would be looked at with a lot more thoroughness than his own. Wang's, for example.

The meeting was held in the Central Lecture Theatre. The Unit Committee—Secretary Wei, Colonel Yue from Internal Security and someone called Chu from the Technical Department—sat behind a long table on the stage. In front of it was a bare wooden chair, then banked rows of seats filled with CID staff.

Secretary Wei stood up and began to speak. He had a thin, scrawny face and a beak-like nose, almost as big as a Westerner's, that had earned him that nickname, Hawk.

"May and June 1989," he said. "Turbulent times. Times during which our loyalty and common sense were put under considerable pressure. But times from which we can all learn—if we are prepared to. We have all submitted self-criticisms, and they will all be reviewed in the coming months. I want to start today with one of particular interest. Will In-

spector Wang Anzhuang please come to the front of the
stage.''

Wang felt his stomach turn. He stood up, and his legs were
weak. The man who had once led a bayonet charge up an
enemy-held ridge walked tentatively to the front of the hall
and sat meekly down on that wooden chair. The silence was
total.

"Comrade Wang has recently concluded a murder investigation with great aplomb . . .'' Wei said, forcing a grin on to
his lips. (Wang grinned back: was he actually going to get
some praise?) ". . . which makes the submission I have here
all the more disappointing.'' The Hawk held up Wang's self-
criticism and turned to the inspector. "Did you really think
you could fool us with this?''

"I'm—not sure what you mean.''

"Yes you are. It was late, but that is excusable. What is not
excusable is its content. Or lack of it. This submission is nowhere near full nor frank enough.'' Wei began leafing through
the pages. Colonel Yue stood up and whispered something in
his ear. They were going to bring up that business with the
gun. A triviality. Let them.

"I have it on the best authority that you accepted a flower
from one of the counter-revolutionaries,'' Wei said instead.
Wang's heart sank. "A flower. Is that true, Comrade Wang?''

"Well, I—''

"Is it true?''

"Yes. I can't see—''

"There's no mention of it here.''

"No . . .''

"Why?''

"It didn't seem significant.''

"Come, come. You are an intelligent man.''

Wang tried to swallow but his throat was dry. How much
else did they know?

"You'd better tell us all about the incident now, Comrade.''

"Yes. Of course.''

The only thing to do was grovel, to admit that he had made
a grave error and beg for understanding. For a moment, a voice
inside him protested. Then he began.

"At that time, I did not realize the true nature of the counter-revolutionary uprising . . ."

The Hawk listened in satisfied silence. When Wang had finished, he nodded his head, then opened the self-criticism again.

"There is also the extraordinary matter of the campfires. Apparently, Comrade Wang, you allowed a group of students to light a campfire, in deliberate contradiction of orders on the subject. I see no mention of this."

"No. I've—been busy. It got left out . . ."

"Tell us about it now, then."

Wang nodded, and began to mumble a second admission. The contrary words pressed forward even stronger, now. The students were almost children; their fires had reminded him more of pioneers at camp rather than sinister counter-revolutionaries. But he fought these thoughts back and stumbled on through his apology.

". . . I admit I was at fault. It was a failure to understand, not a failure of loyalty . . ."

At the end, Wei went into a huddled discussion with his colleagues then got up to deliver judgement.

"I feel Comrade Wang could have spoken with more enthusiasm. We shall be watching him carefully in the next few months. But he does seem to have learnt a lesson. I would remind everyone here that ideological correctness is still the most important part of police work. Superficial concentration on expertise, without due thought for the aims to which expertise is directed, is of little value. Is that message clear, Comrade Wang?"

"Yes, Comrade Secretary." Wang lowered his head.

A smile flickered across Wei's face. Then he turned to the assembled group of policemen and asked: "Has anyone any comments to make?"

Silence. The ordeal was over. All Wang needed to do now was fill in a form, and he would be provisionally reinstated as a Party member and allowed to get on with his life . . . He began to rise from his chair—

"Comrade Secretary!"

The voice came from the back of the hall. A man was on his feet. Everyone turned to see who it was. And gasped; the man was Constable Hong, a former Red Guard now notorious for informing on his colleagues.

"I feel obliged to add a comment, Comrade Secretary," Hong said. "Your information is incomplete. During the period under discussion, Comrade Wang also attempted to prevent members of the People's Liberation Army from carrying out their duties."

Wang felt sick with fear.

"Is this true?" Wei asked.

"I—I don't know what this fellow is talking about . . ."

"I was at Muxudi," Hong went on, "when PLA units met resistance from armed rioters. I distinctly heard Comrade Wang call out to them. He tried to tell the soldiers that the rioters weren't armed. He tried to tell the soldiers to stop defending themselves." Hong paused. "I hate to make such accusation about a fellow policeman, but given the delicacy of the current political—"

Wei cut him off with a wave of his hand. "Comrade Wang, is this true?"

Wang opened his mouth, but no words came out.

"I've got witnesses," said Hong.

"Let the Comrade Inspector answer!"

Still no words.

"Comrade Wang . . ."

The inspector glanced across at Team-leader Chen, who was staring open-mouthed; at Sergeant Fang, who was looking away in embarrassment. Zhao was gazing into space, with that distant expression he seemed to have so often recently. Lu was hiding behind a memorandum. Wang's loneliness was absolute.

For a second, he thought of doing what millions of his compatriots had done in the Mao years: breaking down and throwing himself on the mercy of the authorities. Then he thought of what had happened to them.

He sat down. He looked his Party Secretary straight in the eye. "Are you taking this man's word against mine, Wei?"

The Hawk looked shocked. "Comrade Hong has provided useful information in the past."

"He's a drunkard and a slacker. And now a liar." Wang pointed a finger at Hong and followed it with a glare. The look that came back was as cold and vicious as any cornered criminal. Wang knew he had a fight on his hands.

"I shall prove my case," Wang said quietly. "For the moment I withdraw my application to rejoin the Party. I need time."

"An honest admission now would be much better," Wei replied. "This legalistic rubbish wastes time."

"Maybe. But that is my choice."

"Very well. I think you will find it one that leads you into difficulty. The Party values spontaneous honesty, not the calculated half-truths of intellectuals."

"I'm sure what the Party values above all else is truth." Wang stepped down from the podium and returned to his seat amid a murmur of voices.

16

"Here comes another one," muttered the gatekeeper at the Qianlong. "I wonder what he wants . . . Hey, you!"

The new arrival grinned. "I've come to see Mr. Li."

"With an appointment?"

"No, but I—"

"Piss off!"

A ten-yuan note slapped down on to the windowledge. "Just let me in."

The gateman pocketed the money. "What's your business?"

"My business."

"You won't get past the front door."

Another note.

"Use the service entrance round the back."

Bai Lifan started up the hotel drive.

Fifty or so yards short of the hotel steps, he cut across the lawn, towards the foundations of a "Luxury Olympic-Size Swimming Pool." A couple of workmen stopped to watch him go by, but said nothing. They had already learnt to keep quiet about the comings and goings here.

Round the back, was a huge loading bay. A man in a brown jacket was heaving sacks of rice off a truck. Bai Lifan made as if to speak to him, then a security guard appeared.

"I want to see Mr. Li," Bai told him.

The guard stared back. "He's a busy man. He hasn't got time for the likes of you."

Ten more yuan.

"Wait here."

Bai sat down on a teachest, while the guard went off. Almost without thinking, he checked the lay-out of the place—if it came to a fight, where was it best to be positioned? That crowbar in one corner might come in handy. If they got guns out, he would need to be by that jutting wall . . . Not that he was expecting trouble: his disguise was, as usual, excellent.

Then the guard was back, with a tall man who asked Bai in a coarse Beijing accent what he wanted.

"To see Li. I have something for him."

The tall man looked at him with a sneer.

"From Luo Pang," Bai added.

The sneer vanished. "Follow me."

He led Bai off through a fire door. A lock clicked ominously shut behind them; they climbed a flight of dingy steps and entered a dusty, stone-floored corridor.

"Wait here."

The tall man's footsteps died away. Bai tried to keep calm, but he couldn't help scanning the terrain with a fight in mind. Here there were only exits at either end, plus a trapdoor in the ceiling which mightn't open anyway. No make-shift weapons to hand. Suddenly he felt afraid—there was nothing he could do; he would have to rely on his Tang dynasty plate to look after him. Which, surely, it would . . . Then the footsteps were back. Two sets. Bai looked up at the new arrivals. Li and a companion.

Chao.

Wang—or rather, Bai Lifan—suppressed a gasp. A month or so ago he had stood a few feet from this man. Now they were face-to-face again. Why hadn't George Lim said anything about the scar on Chao's chin?

For a second, Wang panicked. Supposing Lim was part of the conspiracy, too? The game was up—here, now. At least he wouldn't have to face Secretary Wei again.

He took a deep breath. See sense. Triad bosses might have one main bodyguard, but maybe Li liked to alternate. Or

maybe Lim had just made a mistake. No wonder there was so
much crime in America.

Keep calm. Try and get rid of Chao; if you can't, press on.

"Can we talk in private?" he said, putting an extra Beijing
twang in his voice.

Li frowned. "There's nothing you can't show Chao, here.
Who are you?"

"Bai Lifan," Wang replied. "I'm just a small businessman.
But my cousin is a policeman. At a place called Huashan."
He took out the plate and unwrapped it. "He got hold of this.
He told me to bring it to you. He says you'll offer me a good
price for it. Tang dynasty, he says it is."

Li betrayed no emotion in his face, but the way his hands
caressed the plate showed that he knew its worth at once.

"My cousin says there's plenty more where that came
from," Wang went on. "Bigger things, too. Statues, altar-
pieces . . ."

"May we know the name of this cousin of yours?"

"No."

Li glanced back down at the plate. "You should tell me
something. So I can trust you. How did your cousin get hold
of this?"

"Through the chief security officer, Wu. He caught Wu
stealing it: rather than turn him in, he made the fellow tell his
story. Then he decided to get in on the act."

"Careless fellow, Wu. He's dead, you know."

"So I heard. My cousin is eager to replace him."

"He reckons he can do that, does he?"

"Yes. I don't know the details. I don't want to. All I want
is to do business."

"I'll need time to look at this piece, of course."

No. "I'd rather we dealt here, straight away."

"You do, do you?"

"It's a reasonable request."

"Shall I do him over, boss?" Chao put in.

Li paused. Then spoke: "No, Mr. Bai is right. We deal here
and now. My offer is five thousand yuan."

The price was, as expected, derisory. But Wang would have
been more than happy to accept it, to be out of this potential

killing ground. He knew, however, that Bai Lifan would haggle.

"This is economic crime!" he exclaimed. "People get executed for this."

"Six thousand," said Li.

"You know how much this is worth in the West!"

"I know how difficult it is to get it there in the first place."

"A few corrupt customs officers; a student going abroad
with no intention of coming back . . ."

"If you think it's that easy—"

"Ten thousand," said Wang.

Li held up the plate as if he were about to smash it on the
floor. Had Bai overplayed his hand? "Six thousand five hundred," the gangster said.

Wang just wanted this to be over . . .

They eventually settled on seven thousand five hundred; still
an insult, but a lot of money to a petty crook. The gangster
held out a hand for him to shake. Wang breathed a sigh of
relief. Another ordeal over.

"Wait here while I fetch the money," said Li. "Chao will
keep you company."

Or was it over? The boss went off. Chao was staring.

"Don't I know you from somewhere?"

Wang shook his head. "I don't think so."

"I'm sure I do."

"This isn't really my usual business."

"No. Bit of luck that, having a cousin in the police force."

"Everyone needs some luck. That's life."

Chao scowled, subjected Wang to further scrutiny, then
seemed to lose interest. Li returned with the money and
counted it out meticulously.

"Come 'round again, next time your cousin gets something," he said. "Cash payment again: I always keep a supply
handy. Chao, show Mr. Bai to the exit."

The minder did as he was told.

After the stale, devious atmosphere of the Qianlong below
stairs, Beijing was balmy and refreshing. Wang took a great
deep breath—OK, so there was a little pollution—and began
his walk back into town. At the bridge over the ring road, he

paused to watch the traffic and to double-check that the man in the brown jacket was following him. Then he carried on.

The entrance hall of Dongcheng District Number Five Hotel was a narrow corridor perpetually blocked with luggage, customers, rubbish bins and deliveries for the kitchens. Today, two Western backpackers were sitting morosely on the one chair, hoping the receptionist would relent and give them a room. As they hadn't offered a bribe, they were in for a long wait.

Wang pushed his way past and walked up the cold, stone stairs to the fourth floor. He collected his key from the floor attendant, paused to spit into the floor spittoon then let himself into Room 418. It smelt of mould, damp, disinfectant and stale cigarettes. Home from home for Bai Lifan.

He sat down on the rock-hard mattress. It would take the man in the brown jacket a while to find out which room he was in: time to calm down his confrontation with Li. A little deep breathing; a browse through the war comic he had brought for Bai to read—it was all about Yunnan, 1979, and an attack on a Vietnamese-held ridge by a brave platoon commander. What he wanted most of all was a smoke, but Pandas would be a giveaway. Other brands were so disgusting he'd rather abstain. Finally, he took out his wallet and spread seven thousand five hundred yuan out, just to see what so much money looked like. It covered most of the bed.

"Nobody knows I've got it . . ." he found himself thinking. "It's not state money; it came from a crook. Just think what it would buy . . ." He felt guilty at these thoughts, but not as guilty as he expected. That Struggle Session . . . If people were going to brand him a criminal, he might as well start behaving like one. And get the benefits.

The rap on the door shocked him. What had he been thinking?

"Who is it?" he said cautiously.

"A friend of Luo Pang's." Wang scooped up the cash and bundled it under the pillow.

"I need to talk," the voice continued.

"What about?"

"You ought to know. I'm not armed. And I've come alone."

"How did you know I was here?" said Wang.

"I followed you. Look, it's urgent. If you don't open up, you'll regret it."

"In what way?"

"There's someone coming! Just let me in."

Wang did so; the man in the brown jacket burst in and scuttled over to the bed. Only when the door was locked did he relax, pulling out a packet of Flying Horse cigarettes and offering one to Wang. Bai Lifan would have been smoking these vile objects since he was thirteen: Wang had to accept.

"What do you want?" said Wang.

The man lit up too, and seemed to enjoy having a carpenter's rasp shoved up and down his throat. "To do business. Look, I know how much you were offered for that plate—"

"How do you know?"

"Chao told me."

"Why did he tell you?"

"Don't know. He just did. I think he found it funny, your accepting such a small sum. And that's why I'm here. I want to do business with you. Pottery, statues, bronze, silver, gold—anything from that place, I'll buy it. At a decent price."

Wang nodded. "How decent?"

"Double it. I'd have given you fifteen thousand for that plate."

"Really? But what if Li had found out? I've heard he isn't exactly keen on people who betray him."

"That's my problem."

"It could be a big one."

"He's not that clever."

"Isn't he? I've heard he's got contacts with the Yi Guan Dao."

The man looked at him. "You've heard a lot."

"Of course I bloody have. Do you think I'd just walk into that place without finding out as much as I can about it?"

"No . . . What else do you know about Li?"

Cheeky bugger. "Enough not to mess with him. He may have underpaid me, but he gave me cash, there and then—"

"So would I."

"And he doesn't ask as many questions as you do." Wang paused. "If I'm to start double-crossing a guy like that, it's got to be worth my while. Well worth my while."

"It will be."

Wang took another puff. Inhale! "What would you do with the stuff once you got it?"

"That's my business."

"I don't want it being traced back to me or my cousin. Li's organization seems to be cop-proof. How's yours?"

"Solid. And wealthy. Plenty of cash, just waiting to be spent."

Wang let himself appear to be taken in by this simple appeal to greed. "How about some kind of payment in advance?"

The man looked shocked.

"It sounds reasonable to me," Wang continued. "If I'm to trust you . . ."

"I'll—see what I can do."

"Meet me in Beihai Park, tomorrow morning, ten o'clock. With five hundred yuan. Or else no deal."

The man sucked on his Flying Horse. "Tell me the name of your cousin," he said.

"You're joking!"

"I need security, too. If I'm going to cheat on Li . . ."

"I'll tell you in Beihai, once I've seen that money."

"OK." The man glanced at his watch. "Make sure you're not followed there."

"I'll make sure," said Wang.

"You didn't even notice me."

"I'll be extra careful."

"Do that." The man chucked his cigarette on to the floor and stubbed it out with his heel. "Third bench along from the southwest gate."

"I'll be there."

The wart on Bai Lifan's nose came off with a pop. The makeup poured down his cheeks like tears. His clothes became a Western suit, the trainers a new pair of black leather Great Wall shoes. Inspector Wang Anzhuang let himself out of the sordid little room, went downstairs and barged past a group of Cantonese commercial travellers whose addition didn't tally with the manager's. A five minute walk took him to a forty-eight bus stop, where he fought his way on to the first vehicle that came. When it reached Qianmen East Street, he got off.

The sentry saluted him as he went by. But there was an odd look in the fellow's eye, one Wang had seen before—usually aimed at people in trouble. In his office, he found a note from Secretary Wei—*contact me at once*. Wang scrumpled it up and stuffed it in his pocket.

The first light of dawn was trying to creep in through the office window, when Wang put the finishing touches to his report. He'd covered everything he could: Wu's treachery and death, the kidnap of Ren Hui, Jasmine's forced confession, the Yi Guan Dao and their penetration of the Qianlong Hotel. He put the document into an envelope, sealed it and addressed it to the person he reckoned he could most trust in the whole organization: Wheels Chai, down there in the library. To be opened, at once, in case of serious accident.

"Bai Lifan" reached his rendezvous early, refreshed from a few hours' sleep back at the hotel. He found the bench, sat reading his comic—the heroic lieutenant died on the last page, praising the Motherland—then stared out at the lake in front of him. Mandarin ducks, two parks policemen in a rowing boat, down floating like snow from the weeping willows along the shore.

"Good morning!"

The man in the brown jacket—last night Wang had identified him as one Zong Dingfu—was on time.

"Morning," Wang replied. He glanced round to see if Zong was alone. He was. "You've got the money?"

Zong took out a fat manila envelope and handed it over. Wang gave it a squeeze.

"Open it if you want."

Wang did so. Five little bundles of red ten-yuan notes. Genuine, too.

"Now tell me the name of your cousin."

Wang paused, pretending to be searching for a last minute get-out. "His name is Wang," he said finally. "Wang Anzhuang. He's an inspector in the CID."

What would Zong do next? Beihai was a public place: Li's

agent was hardly likely to take out a gun and shoot him. (Wang had come armed, with a non-standard Makarov automatic, just in case.) More likely, he would just smile, chat about business for a bit then report back to the Qianlong. Someone would come and liquidate Bai Lifan later. Possibly the same person whose job it would be to liquidate Wang.

The Triad man nodded his head. "Wang Anzhuang . . . Obviously I've got to check there is such a man there—but I think we can trust each other from now on."

"I'm sure we can," Wang replied.

They agreed on a coded system of communication then parted, each glowing with the satisfaction of thinking they had fooled the other.

The slow train from Beijing pulled into Little River Station. Wang got out, stretched—the train had been crowded, but he wasn't in a position to ask for the use of an official car. A rosy-cheeked woman in an immaculate Chinese Railways uniform checked his ticket; Wang walked out underneath another of those SERVE THE PEOPLE banners and stood in the forecourt. No transport came or went; after a while he realized he would have to finish his journey on foot.

He knew the road out towards Huashan, anyway. It was not long before he was in the country and surrounded by country noises; wind hissing in young wheat, the chug of a water pump, the tinkle of water through a sluice. Men and women were working in the fields, as his family had for generations. Now, he had moved on. To possible disgrace, to undoubted danger.

Another rural sound, an air horn. A shaky, rusting Liberation truck was lumbering up the road behind him. Wang flagged it down. He showed his Police ID, and the driver beckoned him up into the cab.

"D'you investigate murders?" The vehicle clanked into gear.

"Sometimes."

"Any really big ones?"

"They're all about the same size."

The driver went back to chewing his beetlenut with a loud sucking noise. Then he spoke again.

"D'you have anything to do with the Triads?"

Wang felt a shiver of fear. Was this a trap? Surely not. "Sometimes," he replied, trying to sound as offhand as possible.

The man grinned. "I've heard that the Triads cut guy's dicks off and stuff them in their mouths. Is that true?"

"It has been known to happen, yes . . ."

"I've often wondered—do they do it after the victims are dead or before?"

"I'm not sure."

A cyclist wobbled into view, and the truckdriver blasted him off the road with his klaxon.

"In Italy, the Mafia stuff live rats up people's arses."

"Really."

"They don't feed them for a week beforehand—the rats, I mean. They're hungry."

"I'm sure they are."

"Real hungry."

"Yes . . ."

Clank. Another gear change.

"I'd like to be in the police. This job is boring. D'you get to shoot people? Like on Tiananmen Square? Bam! Bam!"

Wang pointed to a farm entrance up ahead. "This'll do fine," he said. "Thanks for the lift."

It was about three kilometres to the Huashan turning then another four up to the camp. At the top of the climb, the ground levelled and the fir trees that filled the bottom part of the valley thinned out. It took Wang over an hour to reach this point; an hour of thought, speculation, anticipation . . . Just where the wood thinned, he noticed an old foresters' hut set back from the track. He walked across to examine it. No, no one had been here for ages. Yes, it was perfect . . . He returned to the track and emerged into the upper valley.

Mount Huashan rose up in front of him—the path, the caves, the summit. Wang suddenly felt a sliver of fear.

Dinner time. Wang sat alone, as he had on his first night here, and surveyed the various groups of eaters. Then, he had been toying with vague suspicions, pulling motives out of nowhere and pinning them on to people, virtually at random. Now he knew what kind of villain he was up against: someone who had entered the City of Willows, who had taken thirty-six oaths of loyalty, drunk the blood of fellow-recruits and hacked a traitor's effigy to pieces. Which one of the people sitting opposite him had done this?

Professor Qiao and Dr. Jian were sitting together for once, discussing some academic topic. Qiao? Most Triads admitted women—one group of female blue lanterns had become notorious during the Boxer uprising—but he could not see this dignified, serious-minded academic joining up. Jian, on the other hand, was still a man of mystery. How did he command all that influence back in Beijing? Through ''patting the horse's arse,'' honest toadying to superiors? Or because of his membership of a powerful, covert organization—like the Yi Guan Dao?

Team-leader Hei Shou sat alone. If he, Wang, were a gangster with orders to kill (as the Triad's Huashan agent surely had), he would sit alone, too. Death demanded that kind of respect. Hei's career was clearly on a downward path—the Triad would offer a new world of power and influence, not to mention wealth.

Then there was Wu's former deputy, Fen. The obvious man to collaborate with Wu, and what better disguise for senior and junior partners in crime than to have their roles reversed on the surface?

Finally, of course, there were Wang's own colleagues. Sergeant Fang, a contented-looking family man. Why had he volunteered to stay at Huashan? To supervise the cover-up of Wu's guilt? Or to be able to get home at the weekend? Inspector Zhao. Ambitious, but on the fast promotion track anyway; a man heading for his own team, for a chauffeur and a house out by the Western Hills. Why throw that away? Team-leader Chen, who had botched this investigation so thoroughly. Jasmine had noticed his photograph . . .

Wang began to eat. The food hadn't improved since his departure. But that wouldn't matter much longer.

After dinner, most people went to the mess hut for a drink. Wang bought CSO Fen a *Tsingtao*, and requested official permission to climb to the top of the mountain. It was granted. Then he joined his colleagues.

"How was the check-up?" Chen asked: Wang had needed some excuse to disappear for a couple of days.

"Fine," Wang replied.

"So you'll be joining us back at our desks," the team-leader went on, "doing proper police work."

"Soon."

"You'll do it now if I say so."

"I need more time. I want to make some observations from the mountain top."

"What of?"

"People's movements."

Chen furrowed his brows in disbelief. Over in a corner, the young patrolman who'd talked about eagles was losing a drinking game and having to make yet another forfeit.

"And eagles," Wang added.

"Eagles?"

"Yes. I have this theory—supposing someone's been training them to take stolen objects to a special place."

Inspector Zhao burst out laughing. Chen began shaking his head. People from another table had put their drinks down and were listening. Wang had centre stage.

"Does anyone have any better ideas?" he said.

"I'm sure it wouldn't take me long to think of some," Dr. Jian muttered at another table.

"Eagles . . ." said Chen.

Wang took out his wallet and produced a fat bundle of ten-yuan notes. "Come on. Drink and sing! *Maotai*, anyone? Dr. Jian? Comrade Hei Shou?"

When Wang said good night and headed back to his quarters, Team-leader Chen came with him.

"What the hell's this all about, Wang?"

"What?"

"Everything. This eagle rubbish."

"It's an idea. I got it from one of the guards on Huashan. Listen to the People, follow the mass line."

"Don't give me that. It's something to do with that Hong business, isn't it? Some kind of protest. Well, I'm not im-

pressed. I had to argue with Secretary Wei to have you kept
on this case. If you don't drop these ideas, I'll suspend you.''

''Just give me a couple of days.''

''Looking at eagles?''

''That's right.''

They walked on in silence.

Chen said: ''And this sudden generosity with drinks . . .''

''I always get a round in!''

''But not for the whole bloody canteen. Where's all this
money come from?''

''Savings. Hong and Wei get what they want. So I figure I
might as well enjoy my last case.''

Chen shook his head. ''It doesn't have to be like that. I'll
stand up for you. Though this eagle thing doesn't exactly make
doing that any easier.''

Wang looked at his team-leader. There had been sincerity
in Chen's voice, and he felt grateful for that. Maybe he should
let his boss in on what was happening.

No. He mustn't take risks.

''Don't just throw it all away,'' said Chen when they
reached the accommodation hut.

''Thanks. Good night, Comrade.'' The inspector laid a hand
on his team-leader's shoulder, then turned away.

Wang carefully packed what he needed for the next day's
vigil, then crept out of his cabin. He had a story ready for the
guard on the gate—but it wasn't necessary; the fellow was
asleep. So much for Fen's security clampdown. And so much
the better . . . Wang walked back to the tree-line and found the
old foresters' hut. His pack made a pillow; the night was warm
so he had no need of blankets; only the insects annoyed him.
But they were much less of a threat than a cornered gangster
with murder in mind. Wang slept well.

He awoke at dawn to the sound of birds, got up and did
some *taijiquan*. Bright sunlight was shafting down through the
trees, and the ancient martial exercises filled the inspector with
simple physical well-being. Man united with nature, the old
Taoist ideal. Then he set off back towards the mountain.

The inspector reached the caves by seven o'clock, surprising
the night-shift with his early arrival. As he sat chatting over a

mug of tea, he glanced idly through the registers to check that none of his suspects had come on to the mountain before him. None had.

He set off again. Out on the cliff-face it was beginning to get warm. He glanced down into the valley. Soon it would be filling with heat like a cauldron.

17

Wang scrambled up the last few yards of the ridge and collapsed in a heap, panting with exhaustion. The summit . . . A glance at his watch, a sip of water, five minutes to recover his breath—then it was time to remind himself of the exact layout of his chosen fortress. He walked to the end of the gully and peered over the end: a sheer drop for hundreds of feet. He climbed the two ridges: no other way up here, either. Perfect.

The thief has to act, he told himself. He's seen me flashing money about; he must reckon I'm up here hunting for hidden artefacts. He alone knows I've got better things to do than make pointless protest gestures. And Li must have told him to—what is it the Triads say?—wash me out. He'll be here.

Of course, he might want do a deal . . . Again, Wang's mind went back to all that money spread out on the hotel bed. And the Struggle Session—the opening skirmish in a war he had little chance of winning. Do a deal? Why not?

To keep such thoughts out of his mind, Wang finished his reconnaissance, tried a practice walk back up the gully covering an imaginary opponent with his Type 77, then set to his final task. It took him about half an hour to build the dummy: a cairn of stones about three feet high across the entrance point where the ridge met the summit, a jacket wrapped round it,

Wang's cap on the top and his binoculars balanced on a stone
jutting out at the front. The final touch: a mask Wang had
bought in Dazhalan Street—of *Wu Sheng*, a minor (and thus
plain-faced) character from Beijing Opera.

Wang stood back and admired his handiwork. He needed to
fluff the jacket arm out a bit more. And raise the collar a
fraction, to hide the corner of the mask. How would "he"
look then, through fieldglasses—or through a telescopic lens?
Perfect.

He left his work of art, found some shade and settled down
into it. He tried to relax—he would, after all, have plenty of
advance warning as his quarry approached. Then a scratching
noise behind him made him wheel round and point a shaking
gun at a small lizard ambling across the gully.

Relax.

He did a few *qigong* exercises to slow his heart-rate. Then
he polished his gun, checked the ammo, glanced at his watch.
Ten A.M. Be patient.

It was getting hot. Wang had brought a groundsheet and a
wide-brimmed sun hat, but the sun was high in the sky now.
The two water bottles he had lugged up here with him suddenly looked inadequate.

Don't drink the first time you feel thirsty, was the golden
rule on survival training. If Wang told his body he was going
to give in straight away, it would soon become agonizingly
insistent. He made himself suffer for at least half an hour before unscrewing the first bottle and sampling the tepid,
metallic-tasting nectar.

Take sips, not gulps. He let the precious liquid trickle down
his throat, relishing every drop. No more till midday.

By half-past eleven, Wang's throat was parched. The sun
was blazing down out of a clear cobalt sky. All the shade that
had greeted him that morning had disappeared; the whole
mountain top seemed to glow with heat. He cursed himself for
underestimating this factor. A voice inside whispered: "Go on,
take a drink now . . ." He reached out for the bottle then pulled
his hand away. Life in the army had taught him willpower: he
was not going to surrender that easily.

Time crawled by. The thirst turned from discomfort to pain, from pain to . . .

"You have to keep alert." That tempter's voice again. "If you need to drink to do that, go ahead. Break your rule."

No.

Drink! Go on.

No.

Suddenly he grabbed the bottle, yanked the top off, took a great gulp of water. Then another, then another, till it was empty.

Soon after, the hoist motor started up. Another curse; Wang had been banking on hearing anyone approach, but this racket would smother the sound. Ten nervous, difficult minutes passed till the motor stopped. The inspector peered down at the ridge.

Nobody there.

Silence returned.

Supposing nobody comes. Supposing they know more than I think they do . . . But how could they? They can't; of course they can't.

Twelve o'clock was time for siesta: only crazy people worked in this heat. Wang stared at the one remaining water bottle that would now have to last him all day. Images kept dancing into his mind, of watermelons, of mountain streams, of the autumn rains in Shandong . . . But this was no time to fight inner battles. Siesta provided the ideal opportunity for his quarry to slip past patrolling guards. Someone might be making their way up the path, right now. All his energy must go on waiting and listening.

Waiting.

Listening.

Nobody stirred in the midday heat. The Huashan valley was as quiet as a tomb.

A noise. Distant, too distant to place or even to recognize. A person on the path below? Then it came again—a clatter of displaced pebbles. Yes: someone was down there.

Wu's boss, the Triad's senior operative at the site of the thefts—the one individual who held the key to the whole business. Wang could hear their footsteps, now.

Then a noise. *Thwack!*

The inspector recognized it at once: a suppressed pistol. A bullet sang past, twenty feet away at least.

Thwack! A second shot shattered the *Wu Sheng* mask and sent the dummy's cap flying into the air.

Wang gasped. Whoever had fired that shot now thought he had just spattered his brains all over the top of Mount Huashan . . . The footsteps grew louder, faster, more confident as the perpetrator came to check his work. Wang's soles and palms itched with excitement. Got you!

Then the fellow spoke.

For a second, Wang couldn't believe it. Of all the suspects . . . But there was no mistaking that voice. Wang looked across at what was left of the mask. The bastard.

"I know you're up there!" the Triad man called out again. But this time, his voice was hesitant. He'd spotted the trap: he knew he'd been outwitted; he couldn't run off the mountain. He would have to come and fight it out.

Wang listened with bitter satisfaction. Then he sprang out from his niche, ran forward to the cairn and dived in behind it. A shot zinged harmlessly past his ear.

"You might as well chuck that gun away and come out with your hands up," he called.

The reply was another shot. The bastard would fight; Wang knew that. He darted out from behind his cairn, saw his quarry taking aim, got in a quick shot of his own and was back behind cover before the next thwack. The Triad bullet hit rock and ricocheted off into space. Well wide.

"You can't win!" Wang shouted.

"Who says?" came the reply. "I can wait as long as you. Longer, probably. How much water did you bring up?"

"Enough," Wang lied. "If I need more, I'll call for it."

"Nobody will hear."

"They'll hear me when I start shooting!"

"They'll think it's me. I told the guards I was coming to finish off those bloody eagles. They think it's a wonderful idea: it took a while to dissuade them from coming too."

Typical of the man. Sharp. But not sharp enough. Wang picked a rock out of the cairn and lobbed it at his adversary's hiding place. It fell short. A second was too long. But he had plenty of supplies. About the sixth or seventh hit home. And the tenth. And the twelfth.

"OK, OK. I surrender."

Inspector Zhao got gingerly to his feet with his hands up.

Why? Zhao had everything; his career was going places Wang's would never go.

"Throw down your gun, Zhao."

Wang knew he should get his captive down off the mountain as quickly as possible, but he was in the grip of raging curiosity.

"Now kick it over the edge."

Zhao did so. It took forever to hit the valley floor.

"Now come up here."

No, Wang told himself. Don't do this. It's not worth it.

Zhao began walking up the path, then the ridge. Wang covered him all the way. When both men were facing each other on the mountain top, Wang made Zhao take off his uniform and throw it across to him; with one hand, he searched through the clothes for weapons, while with the other he kept his pistol locked on his former colleague.

"OK. Sit down. Let's talk."

Zhao said nothing.

"The interrogators in Beijing will get everything out of you. You know how. I'm offering you a choice."

"How nice," said Zhao. Silence. In the distance, an eagle called to its mate.

"Fooled me there, didn't you?" said Zhao.

"I want you to talk."

"Give me a cigarette."

Wang took out a Panda, lit it and tossed it across to his captive.

"I'd like a drink, too. I need one. If I'm going to talk."

Wang handed one of Zhao's bottles back to him. "I want the whole story," he said. "Starting with the murder."

"Murder? Wu fell. You know that, Wang."

"Of Xun Yaochang."

Zhao's face fell. "Why ask me?"

"Because your organization was involved in his death. He was planning to betray you. Who killed him? Ren Hui? Li Dehong? Or was it you?"

"You've got some sort of transmitter hidden somewhere," said Zhao.

"You know how unreliable radios are here."

"A recorder, then?"

"I haven't got time to play games. Get up, let's move."

"Let me finish this cigarette first." Zhao took a puff. "Xun was a piece of scum. I don't see why you're so worried about him."

"Murder is a state crime. As a policeman, it is my duty to investigate his death."

"As a policeman, you have seen better men than Xun tortured and beaten up and sent away to rot in labour camps and—"

"That's no argument and you know it. Did you kill Xun?"

Another puff. "Yes."

A long silence followed.

"Why there, at the opera?"

Zhao smiled. "Because of you."

"Me?"

"You. I was in my office that morning, when the phone went. It was someone wanting to speak to you. I was just about to fetch you—heaven knows why the switchboard put him through to me—but something about the voice made me suspicious. So I said you were out; I said I'd take a message. Xun told me the whole story—he'd joined a gang; he'd become fed up with its petty rules; he wanted to sell us some information about its main operation. Huashan. He knew you were on the case—and that you liked opera, 'cause he did too, and he'd seen you at the People's Theatre. Were you going to be there that night, he asked. I said I knew you were, and that I'd pass a message on. I gave him instructions: he should be in the street outside ten minutes before the show, reading a Martial Arts magazine . . ."

Wang looked horrified.

"The little shit was as good as his word—which made a change," Zhao continued. "I said you'd been detained, which was true; I showed him my ID; I took him to a back-row seat. I wasn't sure how to get rid of him—then you arrived. Time to act fast. The knife trick is one I learnt during the Cultural Revolution: one of the Red Guard groups became famous for getting rid of their rivals that way. Of course, you missed all that, locked away in your Army barracks learning about loyalty to the revolution and patriotism and saluting the Five-Star flag and all that other schoolboy stuff . . .''

"Meanwhile you are a man of the world and throw your lot in with gangsters," Wang snapped. Then he reminded himself that few things suited Zhao more than him losing his composure. "Tell me about the thefts here at Huashan."

"What d'you want to know?"

"Everything. Anything. Starting from the beginning."

"I caught Wu red-handed, carrying a plate on to the upper path. Rather than turn him in, I let him talk. Wu had no plans—no vision—all he was going to do was stick the things in caves and come back years later."

"So you got in touch with Li."

"I set up a proper network for distributing the artefacts. Rather well, I thought. Except that Wu talked."

Wang laughed. "He never said a word. I worked it out. I've got a brain; we do have them in the military, you know."

"But that plate . . . ?"

"I found it."

"Oh, no. Wu and I hid things properly. He told you where it was."

"It was in a crevice in the rock, just below where Wu fell."

Now it was Zhao's turn to look horrified. "It can't have been!"

"That's why Wu fell off the mountain. He was trying to retrieve it . . . My guess is he'd been on the way to one of his worked-out hiding places, when something happened to make him have to turn back. He needed a quick way of getting rid of the plate—and since then, he hadn't had the chance to go and collect it. He began to panic, had too much to drink the night before—"

"Bloody fool!" Zhao muttered.

"He should have told you, shouldn't he? Triad members are supposed to trust one another. But of course, they don't in reality. They stab each other in the back at the first possible opportunity. As your boss did to Ren Hui. Now we're on that subject . . ."

"Ren Hui is scum. He dumps people in the Tonghui River with their fingers and toes cut off—"

"His daughter doesn't."

Zhao fell silent. "No . . ." he said at last. "That wasn't my idea."

"It was your boss's. And it was done to protect you—you and Chao and Zong Dingfu and everyone else in your squalid little organization. Tell me where Ren Hui is being kept."

"I don't know."

"Tell me!"

"I've said, I don't know. Li has several safe houses. Ren Hui could be in any of them. Or he could be in Taibei, sitting by a swimming pool crossing his daughter off his New Year greetings list."

"No. Ren Hui may be a gangster, but he doesn't sink that low. Give me the addresses of these safe houses."

"I don't know them."

"Oh, yes, you bloody well—" Wang raised his arm to strike Zhao—an action which would have suited the captive perfectly. Keep calm. "Any information I want that I don't get here, I'll get the interrogators on to. It's your choice. Tell me about Inspector Liu Qiang."

"Who?"

"The fellow researching into Triad activity."

Zhao looked baffled.

"The fellow who died of a mysterious heart attack just before he was about to look into the affairs of the Green Circle."

"That was silly of him, wasn't it?"

"Did you kill him?"

"I've never even heard of him."

There was something in Zhao's voice that made Wang sure he was telling the truth. Maybe the chain-smoking inspector *had* died naturally.

"What about those thugs in Ren Hui's house? You know about them, I'm sure. You told Li about my plans—then he planted the evidence in Jasmine's desk and sent thugs round to put me out of action and incriminate Ren." Wang pressed the bruise on his side. "I owe you for that, if nothing else."

"No you don't," Zhao replied. The first thing I heard about that whole business was that you were in hospital. I think you'll find I was at Huashan while you were planning your little raid. You should check your facts.'' Zhao shook his head. "You should check your psychology, too. OK, I tried to shoot you up here: you gave me no choice. Until then, I had nothing against you. I enjoyed working with you. I did everything I could to keep you off the track. I didn't want to leave a trail of bodies behind me, especially of people with whom I had no quarrel. I'm not one of these counter-revolutionary villains in one of Lu's comics, who destroys everything and everybody they come across out of spite. I just want what I want.''

"The Huashan artefacts.''

"Freedom.''

Wang puckered his face in disgust. "Your freedom. Other people's suffering . . . Where are the artefacts?''

Zhao shrugged. "I'll leave that one to your interrogators. Or whoever else I choose to tell down there.''

"You don't have a choice.''

"I do. There are people down there eager to talk to me.''

"Like who?''

"The—Minister of Culture.''

"No,'' said Wang. That had been a lie, an improvisation. "There's nobody down there but our interrogators. And if you die before they get the truth out of you, we'll find the artefacts anyway. I know they're hidden in the caves up here. Dr. Jian is searching very thoroughly. He can take his time; he'll find them.''

"He won't. The best pieces left Huashan weeks ago. They're now way beyond your reach, or anyone else's for that matter: Li, Ren, Chao, anyone. The rest of the stuff, I admit, is hidden up here. But you won't find it, and nor will Dr. Jian or anyone else. Wu and I hid it properly. Which is why people down there will want to talk to me.'' Zhao glanced at his watch and stood up. "Shall we get moving? If we hurry, we can catch the Culture Minister before he packs up for the day. He'll be so pleased to hear from me.''

"You're not phoning anyone. This is a police matter—''

Zhao took a step towards his captor. "You can be very naïve, Wang Anzhuang. That's why you've never got on. My back's well covered. Is yours? Secretary Wei and his pal Hong are still after you. Chen can only protect you so far, and after

this farce with the eagles, I'm not sure he'll want to. If anyone's walking back down that path into a bitter sea of suffering, it's you, not me.'' The renegade policeman shook his head
sadly. ''You know, Wang, you belonged with those students.
You should have taken your little scroll with 'Justice' on it
down to Tiananmen Square. You could have all sat around
having a serious philosophical discussion about it—in good
Marxian dialectics, of course—until your Army pals came and
shot them all.''

Wang tried to interrupt. ''That's got nothing to do with—''

''It's got everything to do with the whole damn business.
Why are we both sitting here on this bloody mountain top?
Because of June 1989 and our reactions to it . . . Your feelings
were obvious: your work went to pieces; you had to be parked
behind a desk to keep you out of trouble; your marriage fell
apart. You said and did nothing, however. I don't criticize you
for that; it's an old Chinese story. 'The bird that sticks its head
up is the one that gets shot.' '' Zhao held his fingers out like
a pistol, aimed them at Wang and clicked the imaginary trigger. ''Of course, it's not very honourable what you did, pretending there was nothing the matter—''

''I don't have to listen to this from a murderer!'' Wang
snapped.

''You have to listen to it from someone. That someone has
been you. Now it's me. Quite a relief, I'd imagine. Now, how
d'you think I felt about Tiananmen?''

''I don't give a damn.''

''You do. You have to. You have to know who's on your
side, who's against you—''

''Don't count me on your side. The Yi Guan Dao are a
bunch of gangsters and murderers—''

''And what are the People's Liberation Army, after what
they did at Muxudi?'' Zhao paused. ''What was it like, Wang,
that evening they opened fire? I've only read the internal Party
documents: they're always a bit dry. How did it feel to be
there, to see Chinese soldiers shooting unarmed civilians?
They used Kalashnikovs, didn't they? A 7.62 calibre bullet
with a muzzle velocity of six hundred metres a second, fired
at close range—it must have been messy. Anyone suddenly

turn bright red and fall to bits beside you? Yes, I can see that
they did. Any young girls? Any little round-eyed Chinese children? Or was it just blokes like you and me?'' Zhao paused
again. ''You still dream about it, don't you? Those cubicle
walls are pretty thin. Or is it Chen who shouts: 'Don't shoot!
They have no weapons!' in his sleep?''

Wang tried not to listen, not to take any of this in—but his
ears had begun to ring with the screams of that crowd. He saw
that teenage girl pitch forward; he saw the blood pump out of
her back. He felt that rage rising within himself; helpless, trea-
sonable, unspeakable.

''That . . . doesn't excuse what you've done,'' he mumbled.

Zhao carried on, ignoring him. ''I was disgusted by Tiananmen, too. I wasn't there on the night, but I saw enough to
sicken me. There was a lad who stood in front of a line of
tanks. They had to stop—there were Western cameramen
about. And Chinese cameramen, too: ISB. I was in the station
when they brought him in. He'd been beaten about a bit, but
not as much as later on. Of course, in the end they took him
out and shot him. A braver man than I'll ever be, forced to
kneel down and die in the dust like a dog.

—''That decided for me. Get out. Tell the truth. I didn't know
how; I didn't know when; I just decided. Wu provided my
chance.'' Zhao paused. ''Of course, it could be your chance,
too . . .''

''My chance?''

''To tell the world the truth.'' Zhao smiled. ''Come with
me. To the West. I've a million dollars' worth of stuff in Hong
Kong. Took it over in a suitcase when I went to investigate
that stupid set-up with the Buddha in Canton. We could split
it fifty-fifty. Five hundred thousand dollars each. Look on it
as a reward, for doing what you want to do and what you have
to do deep down—tell the truth.''

''Never!'' said Wang.

''So you don't really care about Muxudi after all?'' Zhao
replied. ''Oh well, that's nice to know. You really are a Party
hack, after all—just like Wei and Hong. Only they're a bit
smarter than you. It's bad luck those two fellows are going to
ruin you, just to suit their vanity and advance their careers a
bit, but that's the way it goes. That's the deal with the Party,

isn't it? It's a monster, but you can hitch a ride on its back; if you happen to fall off and get trampled, you have to keep quiet. It's called being honourable, though heaven knows why.''

"I agree, wrong was done—"

"And I'm giving you a chance to put it right. Justice. Isn't that what you believe in? A chance to speak out. A chance to get even.''

The images came crowding in: the Struggle Session, Hong's face, Muxudi, the dead girl. Wang tightened his grip on his gun. Fight them.

Accept! Half a million dollars. Freedom to speak.

Freedom to commit treachery.

Justice. An end to those nightmares . . .

Fight them!

Decide!

I can't.

Wang was as startled by the noise as his captive. His own gun, going off unintended as his finger twitched on the trigger. The bullet slammed into the rock by Zhao's head. The sound echoed round the valley then died away, swallowed by its all-consuming silence.

Wang spoke slowly. "Inspector Zhao Heping, I arrest you for the murder of Xun Yaochang, for fifty-six counts of theft from Huashan archaeological site, for membership of an illegal organization—"

"You're crazy, Wang. Nobody wants you down there."

"For the attempted murder of a police officer—"

"This is the only chance you'll ever get!"

"For conspiracy to defraud the Chinese people—"

Wang watched Zhao pick his way down the ridge then followed, gun in hand. That was the most difficult part of the journey done.

"You can still change your mind," Zhao told him as he set off down the path.

"Walk."

"Think about what I said. About Muxudi, about the money—"

"One more word, and I'll shoot."

"Who's waiting down there for you? Secretary Wei—"

Wang fired—wide, but it had the desired effect. Zhao continued in silence: the only sounds were the two men's footsteps, the pounding of Wang's heart and the screeching of a nest of eaglets frightened by the shot.

Half a million dollars. Maybe more. Freedom. You can still change your mind . . .

High in the sky, the mother eagle heard the sound of her young and turned to investigate. Intruders! She filled with fury, and dived for the nearest one.

Wang didn't even have time to get a shot in: he had to throw up his hands to protect his face. An instant later, the eagle's claws tore into them. Its beak began hammering at his neck, ripping away a huge chunk of flesh and missing an artery by centimetres. Wang heard the rattle of approaching footsteps.

"Don't try anything, Zhao!"

The footsteps just got closer.

The gun was Wang's only chance. He lowered a hand; the eagle's talons skinned his face right next to his eyes, but his fingers found the Type 77 and jerked at the trigger. *Boom!* The bird gave a yelp of fear and backed off; Wang wheeled round to face Zhao, but a stone smashed into his forehead. For an unspeakable moment, Wang lost all sense of balance. He flung his hands out in a desperate grab to stop himself falling: by chance, one of them found a crevice and locked on to it. As he hit the pathway, the inspector's wrist nearly wrenched out of its socket. Terror gave him immunity from pain; his grip held.

"I'm safe!" something inside him said—then Zhao was upon him, unleashing a punch that drove his stomach up into his ribs. A kick followed, aimed at his groin and only deflected by a flailing leg. A second punch, to Wang's newly-healed rib, doubled him up helpless with agony; a second kick slammed into the base of his spine. Then Zhao was grabbing him, turning him over, rolling his helpless body towards the precipice.

Wang didn't summon the old Taoist maxim of war, it just came to him: use the enemy's strength to defeat him. With his last ounce of energy—the pain was so intolerable that if this failed, he would be happy to die—Wang resisted Zhao's pressure. Harder, harder he pushed back, until he felt his assailant redouble his efforts. A moment of maximum resistance—then Wang grabbed Zhao's wrists and hooked his knees under Zhao's stomach, turning his legs into a lever.

"No!" Zhao yelled. But now it was his turn to lose balance. And he had nothing to grip. His feet swung up from under him. His whole body began cartwheeling over his intended victim with all the momentum he had put into his attack. He shouted again; he tried a last desperate grab at Wang, to drag him down too; he found nothing but air.

"*No!*" Then Zhao was spiralling into the enormous emptiness of the Huashan valley. He was gone; he was in space, weightless like an astronaut. The ground was rushing towards him: the rocks, sharp and solid. Just as they had been for Wu . . . He tried to scream, but the air thundering past seemed to choke him.

Wang watched his ex-colleague fall with a strange feeling of detachment. Impact produced a revolting thud; the body bounced into the air, rolled over and over down the scree slope, and finally came to rest against a boulder.

Still Wang felt nothing. Then he leant over the precipice and was violently sick.

18

"How long am I going to be here this time?" the patient asked.

"Two broken ribs, possible lung damage, severe abdominal bruising, lacerations to face and neck—at least a week. Then a trip to Beidahe to recuperate afterward, if my recommendation goes through."

"That's very kind." People like Wang didn't usually get to visit China's top seaside resort.

"Nonsense. Now, let's get these dressings sorted out."

The inspector lay back and let Miss Lin—or Rosina, as she preferred to be called—get on with her work. She had just finished, when Team-leader Chen strolled on to the ward.

"Visiting hours aren't till two o'clock," she told him.

"This is Party business."

"The patient is not to be disturbed."

"I'm a senior official!"

"I don't care who you are. This is a hospital."

"It's all right," Wang butted in. "He's a friend."

Rosina looked disappointed, but let Chen stay. He came and sat by the bed.

"I hope they're looking after you all right," he said in his official voice. "You deserve the best."

Wang shook his head. "I was only doing my job."

"Honourable sentiments, Comrade. Ones I shall pass on to our colleagues at the next Struggle Meeting."

Wang winced at the thought. In the last few days, Wang had relived his argument with Zhao over and over and over again. The thoughts it had inspired stung him with a pain deeper than his worst wounds; several times he had tried to get out of bed and to run to the open, third-storey window and had had to be restrained—the last time by Nurse Lin. Her gentle touch had done something the rough grip of the ward orderly had failed to do—embarrassed him into inactivity and acceptance.

In that new frame of mind, he had been able to be more objective about the story Zhao had told him up there on the mountain. The CID hadn't been involved in political arrests, that was Internal Security. So Zhao couldn't have seen the arrest of the young man who had stopped the tanks. So the story was a lie. And the emotions that went with it? Zhao's career hadn't nosedived since Tiananmen: quite the opposite. If the fellow had really cared, he would have shown strain, the way Wang had. No, Zhao had lured him into a beautifully-crafted spider's web of lies. And he, Wang, had been the perfect victim.

"I'm afraid our raid at the Qianlong wasn't very successful," Chen went on.

"Not successful?"

"No. The people you told us about—Li, Chao, Zong—had all gone. On a flight to Taiwan, we subsequently discovered. And Li's office was empty: no papers, no antiques."

"How the hell did they know?" Wang muttered.

"No idea," Chen replied.

"When was the raid mounted?"

"Yesterday. As soon as we knew—"

"But I've been here four days. What happened to that file I sent down to Chai?"

"There was some delay."

"What sort of delay?"

"Delay," Chen replied.

"Who took that fucking file?"

Rosina Lin was by the bedside in a moment. "Calm down, Anzhuang. Don't make a scene." She laid a hand on his forehead, then turned and fixed Chen with a glare. "I said the patient was not to be disturbed."

"Yes. I, er, um, I'm sorry, Comrade, I . . ."

"When I say something, I mean it," said Rosina.

Chen grinned with embarrassment.

"I think you'd better leave," she went on.

"No," Wang butted in. "It's my fault. Comrade Chen just had some bad news. He was right to tell me. He must stay. Five more minutes."

Rosina looked at him then nodded her head. "Five minutes. I'm timing it."

"Who took the file?" Wang asked, once she was out of earshot.

"I—I'm not quite sure. Internal Security, I suppose."

"You suppose?"

"Well, I know. Something to do with, er, the stuff that came up at the Struggle Meeting. Look, we're not in a position to alienate senior cadres at the moment. There's that, then the business with Zhao—"

"Are you equating the two?"

"No, no. Of course not. But other cadres . . . I've been working hard, pulling strings, trying to get things back to normal. Which they will be, in time." Chen shook his head. "You wait till you get a team of your own . . ."

"If people like Wei and Yue have their way, that could be a long time." Wang sank back on to his pillows. He stared into space, then asked weakly: "Any sign of Ren Hui?"

"No. We're doing our best. It's not easy, with Li and his friends gone. No evidence; nobody to testify."

"What about Ren Yujiao? She's been released, I take it?"

"There are complications."

Wang shook his head. "Get her out now, Chen. Pull another string. As a favour to me. She's had enough."

The old veteran Da was in his office when Wang walked in.

"Wang Anzhuang! Nice to see you fit again!"

Wang sat down without being asked: the climb up the stairs had been painful. "Thank you, sir."

"You'll join me in some tea? I got hold of some best *tie-guanyin* the other day."

Wang smiled at the irony: Guanyin, the prize heist from Huashan, also gave her name to one of China's premier teas. Colonel Da began to spoon wizened black leaves out of a tin.

"I've come to see you about Ren Yujiao, sir," said Wang, "the girl falsely accused in the Xun Yaochang case."

Da nodded. "Chen mentioned her the other day. But there are problems. She could face charges of deception, perjury, wasting police time—"

"She was trying to protect her father's life, sir."

"He was a gangster."

"To us, yes. To her . . ."

The colonel turned round. "A policeman, like a soldier, cannot be sentimental. Our job is to enforce law."

"Our job is to enforce justice, sir. Ren Yujiao was put in an intolerable position—"

Da was smiling. "Justice. Justice. I like you, Wang. You believe in the sort of things we believed in in Yan'an. Not too many people around nowadays do. I'll see what I can do for this woman . . . Now, about your application."

"Application? For the week in Beidahe?"

"No, to rejoin the Party. I gather there's some kind of delay."

"Yes, sir."

"There shouldn't be. I've arranged to handle the application myself. Wei can't judge character; he always 'takes the black mare for a yellow stallion'—typical of a man who's spent his life behind a desk. I judge people by their actions. If you fill in this form here, I'll make sure you're reinstated to full membership by the time you get back."

The old man held out a piece of paper. Wang took it, stared down at it, then spoke.

"That's kind of you, sir—"

"No need for that. The Party needs you."

"I want a little more time. To consider."

"Consider? There's nothing to consider. If I say you're in, you're in."

Wang paused. "I'm not sure I want to be in, sir."

Silence fell. Which Da broke: "Don't want to?"

"I've been—"

"Thinking?" The old man frowned. "Too much thinking

can be bad for you. You don't know what China was like in
the old days. You've just read books. I was there. I've seen
men starving to death, when there's a landlord in the same
town with a full belly and an even fuller storehouse. I've seen
streets in Shanghai full of prostitutes—Chinese women selling
themselves to foreigners, to pay for opium imported by the
British. I saw that famous sign outside the Shanghai park: NO
DOGS OR CHINESE. The Party changed all that. It made us
stand up. It gave us pride. And it still does.''

"Still, sir?" Wang didn't mean to put it that bluntly; it had
slipped out.

Da said nothing. His face was suddenly expressionless—
what was he thinking? Outside, a siren wailed.

The old campaigner let out a long sigh.

"I was aware of your feelings about June 1989," he said.
"You are not alone in disagreeing with some of the methods
used to restore public order. But that does not give you the
right to desert your duty. Do you love your country?"

"Of course, sir."

"Good. In the old days, there was a stock reply to that—
then you must logically love the Party, too. But I understand
that in your lifetime, the Party has made too many mistakes.
Many of my colleagues didn't survive the Cultural Revolution—do you think I have no bitterness, no anger about that?
But I have my memories of the old China to counter-balance
it.'' Da paused. "You're a young man, Wang. If you want to
change things, you have time. But you won't change anything
outside the Party. All you'll do is knock things down, destroy,
snipe, disrupt. Get back inside, and you can achieve things. I
happen to believe that's the way things should be: you should
serve your country first, change it second. Other people disa-
gree—but the facts are indisputable. Outside the Party, you
have no influence, so your views and values count for nothing.''

Wang nodded his head. Inside, a kind of war was going on.

"I'll make it easy for you," the old man continued. "One
of Minister Tao's under-secretaries is the daughter of an old
friend of mine. If I get your form on my desk by tomorrow,
properly filled in, of course, I'll phone her and tell her to get
the Ren woman freed. It might take a few days—she's not

that powerful—but it will happen.'' Da paused. ''If I don't get that form back, then I'm afraid you will be campaigning on your own, for Ren Yujiao and for yourself. I know Wei and that little shit Hong are after your blood. I dislike people like them almost as much as you do—but if you won't serve your country any longer, then I can't keep them off you. I'm sorry to be so brutal, but it's called realism.''

Wang looked up at his photographs. Wan and Yi, grinning at a Seagull camera. Men who had died for their country. And their beliefs.

Zhao's words: ''The Party is a monster.'' The words of a traitor—but how apt they had sounded. Then. Now?

He thought of Da: ''You won't change anything outside the Party.''

And of Jasmine Ren. ''Can I trust you?''

Decide.

Wang's eyes rose to the top of his bookcase. Of course. He crossed to the shelves; he took down the *I Ching* and its accessories; he set up the incense burners and the sticks. He kowtowed, broke the smoke-path three times, took up the forty-nine yarrow stalks and began the slow process of building up a hexagram.

Yin, Yin, Yang—a mountain below. Auspicious. Then above it, *Kun*, earth. That made hexagram 15, *Qian*, modesty. ''He who is great of spirit disciplines himself with humility. Ever modest, ever retiring, he fords the greatest river. Success!''

Wang bowed his head. He wondered how many other Chinese officials had faced the same dilemma, and how many had consulted the same oracle and got the same answer. In three thousand years there must have been a great many.

His first evening at Beidahe, Wang hardly touched the banquet spread out before him. They had top chefs at the Number Six Party Guest Lodge, but the new arrival wasn't interested. He remained silent during his meal, too, leaving as soon as possible and walking painfully along the beach. He found a rock and sat there, watching the sun set behind the roofs of the resort.

Modesty. Not weakness. He had done the right thing. Or
had he?

Next day, Yellow River carp in ginger tempted him to eat;
the next day hunger drove him—and it was delicious, he had
to admit. He talked a little, too. The fellow sitting next to him
was also a policeman, a commissioner from Yunnan province.
They discussed the Vietnam war, drugs, many of which flowed
through the southern province, and the difference between a
policeman's life in the big city and in the provinces. Suddenly
it all seemed normal. He thought of that moment at the Zhengyang Gate, waiting for Lu. Life goes on. And an innocent
woman was free.

That evening, sitting on his rock again, Wang felt something
he'd almost become a stranger to: pride.

Lunch time on his first day back at work. Chen had been
briefing Wang all morning on a series of armed raids on sub-
urban shops; the inspector felt the need for fresh air and went
out for a walk. Out on to Qianmen East Street, left up Justice
Avenue, past the gate of the Internal Security Bureau.

He didn't recognize Dr. Jian until he was a few yards away.
The young man was striding along the pavement, muttering to
himself and kneading his palm. Wang thought of greeting him,
then turned away, waited till Jian was past and began to follow. Just out of curiosity.

The young academic turned into the *Ke Ge Bo* gateway.

Wang gasped in horror. Jian spoke to the guard, then waited
while the latter went into his cabin to make a phone call. Then
the doctor was waved through.

Wang walked up to the gate. The guard looked at him suspiciously: Public Security uniform counted for little here.

"Do you have an appointment, Comrade?"

"No," Wang replied. "But I wish to see Colonel Yue. Ur-
gently."

"Yue?" The look of surprise that flashed across the guard's
face told Wang all he needed to know.

"I guess that fellow's got there first."

The guard did nothing to contradict him. "I can put a call
through if it's important."

Wang shook his head. "That won't be necessary. I'm sure the doctor will tell the colonel all he needs to know."

Wang went straight back to his office, locked the door and took the phone off the hook.

So Dr. Jian spied for Internal Security. No wonder he was so immune to criticism! And no wonder he had invented that story about the snooper—to cover up for the fact that he was the one who had been snooping on other people.

So why were Internal Security so interested in the Huashan thefts? No obvious reason. Except the usual criminal's one.

A deal. The Triad needed protection. Someone on Justice Avenue wanted a cut of the profits. That same someone had tipped Li off, enabling him and his cronies to get away.

And what about the events at Pickaxe Alley? If Zhao hadn't told the Triad about Wang's planned search, who had? Who, apart from Wang, Lu and a couple of surveillance men, had known about it?

Internal Security.

Who could have persuaded Minister Tao to let the Frenchman in Canton go free? Who could have scared Inspector Liu Qiang the Triad-hunter, so much that his weak heart had given out?

Internal Security.

And Zhao: who had Zhao been planning to deal with when, he got off the mountain? Not the Culture Minister; that had been a lie. But Internal Security? Yes. And—Wang slapped his forehead; how stupid he'd been!—Zhao had been there before. Long enough ago to have seen the arrest of a young man who had stopped the tanks on Tiananmen Square. He probably hadn't given a damn about the fellow, but he had seen him, and remembered.

Wang wondered how the conspiracy had come about. Zhao must have contacted Yue—his former boss?—after joining the Triad, to buy himself official protection. The convolutions made Wang shudder. Were there any traces he could follow, any evidence he could unearth to prove his case?

He stared down at the diagram he had drawn. There were no participants, apart from those in the ISB, left in the country. No stolen items had been recovered; nothing to subject to forensic tests. Getting at ISB records would be impossible—and, anyway, if Zhao had a file there, it would have been destroyed by now.

Dr. Jian. Arrest him! Use all those tricks, the ones Wang hated, the cow-prods, the truth drugs, the truncheons, the electrodes.

No point. The doctor had just been a stooge, a paid informer. Probably blackmailed into so being. He would know nothing of use. And even if Wang did arrest him, the order would be countermanded at once. Jian would "disappear" soon after. Wang would have more impossible questions to answer.

Go to Colonel Da; tell him the whole story. He had rescued Wang from Secretary Wei; he hated corruption, too; he was a fighter.

But that was precisely why Wang couldn't tell him. The old campaigner would fight—and lose. Wang would be destroyed with him.

"Bastards!" Wang said to himself as he tore the paper up into long, thin shreds.

"Bastards!" he repeated as he tore the shreds into tiny squares.

"Bastards!" The squares tumbled from his hand into the wastebin like snow. Inspector Wang Anzhuang sat and stared at his scroll.

Zheng yi. Justice.

For the small and weak only, for people like Wu and Zhao. (No need for any guilt about his ex-colleague, now; Yue would have killed the fellow the moment he ceased being useful.)

"Bastards!"

Eddie Zheng met his special guests at the bottom of the drive.

"I've reserved the best seats in the house!" he told them.

The man, a policeman aged about forty, looked haggard and pale. He forced a smile on to his face. The woman, younger than he and a great deal more cheerful, grinned easily.

"It's the least I could do after what you did for Jasmine, Inspector," Eddie went on. "She told me all about it, when she came to say goodbye."

"Goodbye?"

Eddie's face fell. "She's gone abroad."

"I thought you said she wasn't the type to desert her homeland."

"It unbalanced her, this business with her father." Eddie gave a shrug of resignation: Wang wasn't the only person to have become worldlier in the last month. "She can start again in Taiwan. With her talent, she'll go far."

"Taiwan?" A smile stole over Wang's face. Had someone told her about Li's escape? Maybe the Shan Master wouldn't escape justice after all.

They began to walk towards the hotel.

"Er, you haven't introduced me to your lady friend," said Eddie.

"Oh, sorry, this is Lin Xiangyu. Though I guess you'll prefer to call her Rosina."

Eddie shook her hand and grinned from ear to ear, his usual reaction to an attractive woman. They walked a little further.

"That looks smart," said Rosina, pointing at the new pool.

Another grin from Eddie. "Yes. It's Olympic-size. I can get you tickets if you like. When it's finished." He flushed with pride. "D'you know, a month ago that was just a patch of lawn! Then they dug this hole, poured in tons of cement—"

"Cement?" Wang cut in. "When was that?"

"About three weeks ago. Maybe two."

"Cement . . ."

"We've got a gala opening in a fortnight," Eddie went on. "You must be my guests!"

"I'd be delighted," said Wang. "You'll come, won't you, Rosina?"

The woman nodded acceptance.

Of course, Wang could order the pool dug up, but the Tourism Ministry would create havoc. And what use was a dead body when the killers were in another country with which there was no diplomacy, let alone extradition? Jasmine appeared to have guessed the truth about her father, anyway.

They reached the hotel entrance. The doorman bowed obsequiously; the lift took them up to the twentieth floor. TONIGHT IN THE STARLIGHT SUITE! TRADITIONAL CHINESE SILK AND BAMBOO MUSIC.

Eddie showed the guests to a front table. Polite applause from the small but select audience greeted the two performers, both men in their fifties, one with a reed flute, the other with a *qin*, a seven-stringed dulcimer that hadn't changed in two and a half thousand years since Confucius had mastered it. They announced their first number in Chinese and broken English, and began to play.

Wang's thoughts went back to Yue and the Triad, as it had for the whole of the past week.

Find some proof!

There isn't any.

What kind of policeman does that make you, then?

A human one. A real one . . . Wang looked across at Rosina. She was smiling, enjoying the music—unlike Eddie, who had already begun to fidget. And suddenly the inspector's anger was gone. Those artefacts, even the beautiful Guanyin: hadn't they caused enough misery? Let them stay in their hiding places! And as for the ones Zhao had spirited away—the villains weren't going to get their hands on those, either. Yue had quite possibly got nothing for his intrigues and certainly would get no more. Tomorrow, Wang would distribute a memorandum suggesting that further searches of the upper caves were a serious waste of manpower. The path beyond the site should be dynamited. Copies to Chen, Wei, Da, Minister Tao.

And to Colonel Yue. A hint to the corrupt cadre: I know. And if any harm comes to me, the world will know, too.

Old Wang would not have approved of such deviousness. But his father had belonged to a simpler, older world. Now you had to fight hard and sometimes dirty; now you had to give trust sparingly; now you had—he looked across at Rosina—to care for those who cared for you, not for abstract theories or the words of ancient sages. An improvement? Wang doubted it. But the *I Ching* had told him to accept reality. His mind went back to Constable Lu, and the first time the lad had come to visit him in hospital. Wang had felt afraid for Lu's old-fashioned simplicity. It hadn't been Lu he had needed to fear for, but himself.

Now, he need fear no longer.

•   •   •

It was just another evening at the Golden Lotus Club. The young Englishman who had come in an hour ago was now sitting in the corner, telling Lily Wong about reinsurance and how important it was to the world economy. They finished their bottle—the club was almost out of '66—then Lily crossed the dance floor. The youngster followed her, eager and nervous. His first night with a hooker! They went upstairs; Lily opened the door of her little room; the Englishman stood hesitantly on the threshold then followed her in. As he sat on the bed, he felt more scared than ever.

"So this is your pad, eh?" he said, grinning idiotically.

Lily smiled back. Plenty of time.

"That's a nice picture," the youngster continued, pointing up at the mantelpiece. "Jolly nice."

Lily kept smiling. "It's an ancient Chinese goddess. Guanyin. She looks after people—poor people, the weak, the sick."

"Right . . ." The young man had been brought up to regard such concerns as soft and contemptible, but they suddenly seemed the most important things in the world.

"I have a shrine to her in my home," Lily went on. "A friend gave me a statue of her."

Amongst other things that her Comrade from Beijing had given her: plates tiles, brasswork, parchments with ancient characters on. He'd promised her he'd be back to collect them, but he had never appeared. All he'd sent her was some kind of sketch with clusters of figures and strange, snaking diagrams on it. *Map of Mount Huashan Caves*: what the hell did that mean? Still, she'd keep it safe. It might be worth something one day.

Lily watched as the young Englishman began undoing his clumsy lace-up shoes. If Zhao didn't turn up, she would sell all the things he'd given her. Except Guanyin. If they turned out to be valuable, she could give up this life. Buy a bar herself, maybe—but not in Hong Kong, not with the Communists coming.

GLOSSARY

Ai-ya!	Exclamation of (usually unwelcome) surprise
Beidahe	Exclusive seaside resort
Blue lantern	Triad recruit
Cadre	Senior Party official
CCTV	China Central Television
Chongwen	Poor area of Beijing
Dazhalan	Alley at centre of Beijing's commercial area
Erhu	Ancient musical instrument
Ganbei!	Cheers!
Guanyin	Buddhist Goddess of Mercy
Han	(a) Ethnic Chinese (b) Ancient dynasty (c) common surname
Huashan	(Fictional) mountain north-west of Beijing
Hukou	System of local registration
Hutong	Alley
I Ching	Ancient Chinese method of divination
ISB	Internal Security Bureau (Secret police)
Jiao	Small unit of currency (one tenth of a yuan)
Jiaozi	Meat-filled dumplings popular in Beijing
Jinan	City in Shandong province
Jingju	Beijing Opera
Kangxi	Qing dynasty emperor
Ke Ge Bo	Street slang for Internal Security Bureau

Lao Tzu	Founder of Taoism
Lei Feng	Ideal Maoist soldier, "goody-goody"
Maotai	Clear, strong alcoholic drink
Ming	Dynasty (1368–1644). Also surname
Muxudi	Bridge in Beijing. Site of massacre, 2–3 June 1989
Nanping	Village in rural Shandong province; Wang's birthplace
PLA	People's Liberation Army—Chinese armed forces
Qianmen	Front Gate of old Imperial city
Qianlong	Qing dynasty emperor. Also luxury hotel in Beijing
Qigong	Ancient Chinese art of meditation and physical exercise
Qing	Last imperial dynasty (1644–1911)
Qipao	Skirt with slit down one side
Red Cudgel	Fanatical teenagers in Mao's Cultural Revolution (1966–76)
Red Guards	Enforcer in Triad lodge
Renminbi	Ordinary "People's" money (foreigners have special "Exchange Certificates")
Shandong	Rural central/northern province
Sancai	Tang dynasty pottery style
Shan Master	Boss of Triad lodge
Song	Dynasty (960–1279)
Sun Tzu	Author of classic book on strategy, the "Art of War"
Taijiquan	Ancient Chinese keep-fit/meditation exercises
Tang	Dynasty (618–907)
Tsingtao	Chinese beer
Type 77	Standard-issue Chinese service handgun
Wanchai	Red-light district of Hong Kong
Willow City	(a) Term for Buddhist heaven (b) Triad lodge
Wu Sheng	Character in Beijing Opera
Wushu	Martial Arts
Xinhua	Chinese State News Agency. De facto Chinese Embassy in Hong Kong
Yan'an	Communist stronghold during Civil War;

	symbol of Party loyalty and comradeship
Yang, Yin	Basic principles of Taoist cosmology
Yi Guan Dao	Northern Chinese Triad
Yuan	Basic unit of Chinese currency
Yunnan	Province bordering Vietnam, site of 1979 Sino-Viet war
Zhang	Most common name in China
Zhengyang	Gate at south end of Tiananmen Square
Zheng yi	Justice